THE GOOD

THE BAD

and

THE BLUE

M. Triplett

H. Triplett

DEDICATION

I dedicate this book and give a very heartfelt tribute to all the slain victims of police brutality, racism, and abuse of power who are now our angels watching over us. We shed tears for your loss, we miss you, and we want you to know that we are here to tell your story

I dedicate this book and thank all the brave police who live by the code of humanity and who uphold the code they have taken even if it means challenging the status quo in the ranks of their own police department. These individuals know that their main purpose is to help preserve life—not take it.

CONTENTS

ACKNOWLEDGMENTS

I want to thank my wife and editor, Gina Ferguson for putting in the long hours and hard work to help me tell a story that needed to be told.

I want to thank my brother and co-author, Haven Williams for his brilliant ideas and invaluable research that he poured into this epic story.

I want to thank Cesar Marenco and Derek Parker for giving me their insight on this novel. Thank you gentlemen.

The Good, The Bad, and the Blue takes a bold broad look at how slavery, racism, and occupational power have manifested in our society and have become the underlying causes of today's issues between civilians and law enforcement. The authors analyze the violence and death that occurs when black civilians are confronted by white police and they also focus on the unjust harassment, shooting and killing of civilians by police on a whole. The storyline contains an investigation of the anger, fear and distrust the public has towards police and includes an in-depth look at how this has resulted in retaliation and additional casualties on both sides.

An examination is done to determine whether police conduct alone is the reason our society is in this position today. Does any of the responsibility fall on politicians and leaders who run each city? Does any of the responsibility fall on the victims? Does any of the responsibility fall on influential leaders in our society?

The authors use data, facts and theories to present explanations and offer solutions on how to end the senseless loss of life that is occurring in our country and they provide ideas that can redefine the interaction that should exist between civilians and law enforcement.

Once you read The Good, The Bad and the Blue, you will be compelled to become an honorary soldier in the reconstruction movement, that will save our society.

The facts and opinions in this book will hold everyone from Hollywood to the 'Hood' accountable. We will all have to look at ourselves in the mirror and face the damage being done to our community, society, and country.

We can fix it, but we have to realize what we have done wrong, have transparent conversations, be open to change, and make that change a reality. The survival of our country depends on you.

If you are already doing what you can to help – your country thanks you. If you are doing nothing, your country needs you. If you are part of the problem, your country is asking you to change.

TO THE BLACK MEN READING THIS BOOK

You most likely will not agree with everything you read, like when you learn that Michael Brown was shot in self-defense. But keep an open mind. The goal of the information is to open your eyes to the data and facts in an attempt to save your life. Those of you filled with anger who want to take up arms should know that doing that, will not solve the problem.

TO THE BLACK WOMEN READING THIS BOOK

If you are a black woman who understands her role in this controversy and you are prepared to help, this book may provide you with information that may save your life. If you are married to a black man, you may need to lead the journey down the road of change to help save his life.

TO THE WHITE WOMEN READING THIS BOOK

Like the Black Woman, you play a critical role in bringing the house back to order, but you need to own it. If you see something wrong, stand up and say something. If you see something right, be a cheerleader.

TO THE WHITE MEN READING THIS BOOK

If you are already helping to right the injustices being seen today – we thank you. If you are doing nothing, it is time to get involved. You are a change agent and we need your support to fix the treachery that some people want to impose on black people in particular, and on society as a whole. Once you get involved the world will thank you.

TO THE MEN AND WOMEN IN BLUE READING THIS BOOK

If you represent the oath you took before you received your shield and weapon, you are probably already not happy about the reputation that the blue community has today. The facts presented in this book may make you more distressed about how your "family" is characterized. The one thing you should know is that the pathway to change – starts with you.

REFLECTIONS OF THE PAST

Darkly pigmented flesh from birth

Straight into the arms of death

Daddy mad as hell, Mama—No love left

As a child, nothing made sense

But I quickly learned the deal

Some of us worked in the house, some of us in the field

The regulators, land-owner, and people who got paid

Lived good, were mean as hell

and all were a lighter shade

Not sure what going on, haven't seen daddy in a while

Land-owner visits a lot and Mama made another child

A small dirt floor shack is the place I called residence

Andrew Jackson you need to fix this

It's your duty as president

I'm dead and gone now, you will never see me

Its 1835, they called me Great Grand Daddy

Still feeling the effects of the Willie Lynch letter

The Thirteenth Amendment in place

and things still not better

Every day is still a struggle I feel it in my flesh and bone

I'm free, but eating scraps and struggling on my own

Others have found a way to live in this time

much better than me

Like my distant relatives thriving in Boone County

The good times came to an end though

things had gotten too good

So they all got thrown out of town

go find your own hood

A small room in a public house

is the place I called residence

Theodore Roosevelt you need to fix this

It's your duty as president

I'm dead and gone now, you will never see me

Its 1905, they called me Grand Daddy

Survival still difficult, to me that's no new thing

My hope for equality rests with Martin Luther King

New day, new page, still things ain't right

Not like Grand Daddy had, but still the same fight

Free to roam, free to live

freedom reign from the mountains

Still can't eat at some counters

or drink from some fountains

Now I'm starting to learn, I'm reading books

My people still branded as criminals and crooks

My new knowledge set me right though

it's a brand new day

Every now and then I catch a beat down

so I stay out the way

A small project apartment is the place I called residence

Gerald Ford you need to fix this

it's your duty as president

I'm dead and gone now, things still kinda bad

Its 1975, they called me Dad

Life is much better, lots has changed My

people in the movies, in sports, on stage

I graduated from college, I have a family, life is good

Multicultural melting pot describes my neighborhood

No longer day to day waiting for the boom

But sometimes I still feel the pain

of my ancestors' wounds

There still a problem though, I see it in the news

People like me getting killed by the people in Blues

Who's right, Who's wrong, I am not really concerned

But it needs to get fixed

before the next generation learns

The hate, the racism, the pass down from the adults

And you goddamn right, it will be all our fault

Before you pull that trigger I need you to think

We need Black lives to matter before they go extinct

I live in a house like yours

this is the place I called residence

Barack Obama you need to fix this

It's your duty as president

I'm dead and gone now, I'm the victim of a gun

Its 2015, and I was your Son.

REMEMBER ME

Sean Bell, 23

New York, NY

Killed: November 25, 2006

Crime: On the night before Bell's wedding, Bell and his friends attempted to flee the scene of escalating tension with the police. The police fired about 50 shots into Bell's car, killing him in the process:

Aftermath: All three officers were acquitted on all charges. They and their commanding officer were fired/forced to resign. New York City agreed to pay Bell's family $3.25 million to settle their wrongful death suit.

SEAN IS WHY BLACK LIVES NEED TO MATTER

1

CLOAKED WITHIN

"Fifty years ago we'd have you upside down with a fucking fork up your ass." .... *you're brave now motherfucker. Throw his ass out. He's a ni**er! He's a ni**er! He's a ni**er! A ni**er, look, there's a ni**er."*
[1]

-*Michael Richards*
Hollywood Actor

Today, the relationship between police and black people is in tragic disarray. From the late 70's through the 90's one would only periodically hear about a case of police abuse where the police overstepped their authority. For example, one of the most memorable police abuse cases of the time was the 1991 Rodney King beating. It seemed that cases like this were few and far in between up through the millennium. We now know that this was only perception and not reality. We just weren't getting all the information about what was happening because news and media were not as accessible and far-reaching as they are today. It is 2018 and nowadays seems like we hear about an unjust case of police brutality every few days or so. There appeared to be a tidal-wave resurgence of hate that occurred around 2012. What happened to set this kind of hate in motion? Maybe this is the wrong question. Perhaps the question that really needs to be asked and answered is did the relationship between police and black people ever really get better since slavery?

From news media to social networks we see black people being killed by police for minor infractions that get escalated and blown out of proportion. For example, there is no reasonable expectation that someone will be killed over a broken tail-light. I for one don't want to live in a society like this, especially when we have real criminals who need attention.

We also see police in riot gear attacking young innocent teenagers on private property. What message does this send to the younger children watching? How is this going to improve police-community relations?

This is unacceptable in America, especially when our politicians continually make the point that this is the land of the free and home of the brave. The ring of truth of this assertion is starting to get tarnished by police conduct against American citizens. The legislative conflict between police forcefully moving children from private property and the First Amendment right of Assembly is on trial.

This First Amendment guarantees freedoms concerning religion, expression, assembly, and the right to petition. It forbids Congress from both promoting one religion over others and also restricting an individual's religious practices. It guarantees freedom of expression by prohibiting Congress from restricting the press or the rights of individuals to speak freely. It also guarantees the right of citizens to assemble peaceably and to petition their government.[2]

I once served in the military and I remember a time when I would allow nothing to get in the way of my allegiance to my country. I would have jumped on a landmine to save lives, rushed a hill to capture the enemy and sacrificed my life without a thought. All it would have taken was an order from my superior. This personal experience has helped me realize that Police are most likely following orders when they put on their riot gear and brutally abuse teenagers who are having a peaceful rally. As far as I am concerned, this does not excuse them, but the bulk of the blame goes to their superiors. The challenge to change this misguided action must be presented to the Mayor and Police Commissioner who run the city. This situation is beyond critical. Your citizens are being killed – Do something!

Politicians like to quote the famous Emma Lazarus poem on the Statue of Liberty that welcomes immigrants to America. The poem which begins "Give me your tired, your poor, your huddled masses yearning to breathe free..."is inscribed on a bronze tablet that hangs inside the statue's pedestal. I can only imagine that after hearing about some of the tragedies that have happened to immigrants that other immigrants may be having second thoughts about coming to America. One such case was the murder of Amadou Diallo.

It occurred on February 4, 1999, when Amadou Diallo, a 23-year-old immigrant from Guinea, was shot and killed by four New York City Police Department plain-clothed officers: Sean Carroll, Richard Murphy, Edward McMellon and Kenneth Boss. The officers fired a combined total of 41 shots, 19 of which struck Diallo, outside his apartment at 1157 Wheeler Avenue in the Soundview section of The Bronx. The four were part of the now-defunct Street Crimes Unit. All four officers were charged with second-degree murder and acquitted at trial in Albany, New York. [3]

What cultural manifestation has brought us to the point where it is acceptable to take a black life without real consequences and why has this not been challenged and changed? There are three theories that may possibly answer this question.

Retribution Theory

The first reason why police brutality exists is called Retribution Theory. The principle of this theory tells us that the sins of the past and accountability for those sins never really goes away. The responsibility for slavery and the treachery that slave owners imposed on blacks has been passed from generation to generation like the amino acids and building blocks in DNA. It is ingrained deep within slave owner ancestors. Subconsciously some slave owner ancestors falsely believe that slave ancestors will always be a threat and are out to get them back for the hate and murder spelled out in our history books. This psychological mirage results in irrational behavior and manifests itself by making each and every black man, woman and child a threat.

A simple experiment was done by a socially conscious group in order to support the basis of this theory. In a town where it was legal to openly carry a weapon, the group planned to have a young adult white male walk down a main street in broad daylight carrying an AR-15 rifle in a shoulder holster. The plan was to see how police would engage him and then they planned to repeat the experiment with a young black man doing the exact same thing.

After walking about half a mile the white male was finally approached by police. When police arrived they stopped in the street and approached the suspect. Once he was within speaking distance, the officer immediately asked for identification. The suspect refused to give it. The officer then asked "Is there any reason why you are carrying an AR15?' The suspect replied "I'm just exercising my constitutional right." The discussion continued and the video faded out and cut to the young black man walking down the street. Besides the obvious difference of skin color, all things were equal down to the way the black man was carrying the rifle. This time the police approach was much different.

The officer stopped his vehicle about thirty feet away from the suspect and exited his vehicle with the driver's side door open as a shield with his gun drawn.

As he aimed his gun at the suspect, in a loud deep voice he yelled "down!" The suspect lay on the ground and the officer kept the gun on him for five minutes until another officer arrived. When the other officer arrived he approached the suspect and handcuffed him. A third and fourth police car approached. One was a canine unit. An officer from the third police car took the weapon into his possession.

After seeing this experiment, which I would not advise anyone to try because you could be killed and it wastes valuable police officer time, I was left to answer my own question of why the police reacted so differently to each situation. The easy answer is that there were different officers involved, so it is not strange that there were procedural differences. The more difficult answer and more uncomfortable reason for the disparity was that the white police officers felt that the black man was more of a threat than the white man.

Invisible Empire theory

The second reason why police brutality exists is the Invisible Empire Theory. The principle of this theory tells us that there is a small secret sub-group of officers that exists within the underbelly of each police organization who embrace racism against black people. These officers are damaging the public image of good police officers and ruining the reputation of police departments as a whole by promoting their hateful beliefs behind the blue uniform.

This sub-group of officers is extremely dangerous because like all officers, they have been given the legal authority to kill. With that authority and a blue culture that stands by its members under almost all circumstances, they know that they can take a black life and there is high probability that, traffic duty, desk duty, or unpaid leave are the worst punishments they will face.

American History helps to put this theory in perspective. In the early 1900's a group called the Ku Klux Klan was at the peak of its power. The group's initial main purpose was to do everything and anything to suppress political and economic equality for blacks. Why they would waste their time worrying about a group of people who had been held captive as slaves, and who had very little opportunity for financial or educational advancement given the circumstances, was not clear. Perhaps it was that members of the Klan were former slave masters and feared retribution? Or was it that slave owners and the white establishment were worried because they had seen slaves remain resilient and survive after everything they had endured?

Maybe it was the fact that slaves showed signs of intelligence that would easily become brilliance once cultivated?

Regardless of the primary reason or reasons, the psychology of why the Klan hated and killed black people essentially came down to one word – FEAR!

Fear of Retribution

Fear that black people were not inferior

Fear that black people were decent human beings

Fear that black people could think and were intelligent

Fear that their views would one day be questioned

This fear was so special that in the 1920's the Klan membership exceeded 4 million people nationwide! It was so deep rooted that even black children and black elderly adults were not spared. They too were Klan victims, as black institutions like school and churches eventually became acceptable targets to help them carry out their suppression campaign.

Despite many horrific acts of cruelty against black people, members of the Klan were rarely prosecuted. A few key reasons they were not held accountable for their crimes came down to the fact that there was an abundant number of Klansmen who were judges, lawyers and police officers. Other people in these professions who were not part of the Klan did not pursue prosecution of crimes committed by Klansmen because they were worried about their own fate if they had prosecuted a member.

None of this was known to the public because the Klan was known as the "Invisible Empire of the South." Secrecy was maintained for the closed society by the hoods they wore when committing crimes. When in public, they blended in by working within large powerful organizations such as the district courts or law enforcement.

REMEMBER ME

Amadou Diallo, 23

New York, NY

Killed: February 4, 1999

Crime: Mistaken for a rape suspect.

Aftermath: All four officers were charged with second degree murder and acquitted at trial. In March 2004, a lawsuit against the city was settled for $3,000,000.

AMADOU IS WHY BLACK LIVES NEED TO MATTER

The Klan primarily wreaked havoc on black people up through the early 1900's until its revival in 1915 when they also started to target other nationalities and religions.

> *In 1915, white Protestant nativists organized a revival of the Ku Klux Klan near Atlanta, Georgia.... This second generation of the Klan was not only anti-black but also took a stand against Roman Catholics, Jews, foreigners and organized labor. It was fueled by growing hostility to the surge in immigration that America experienced in the early 20th century along with fears of communist revolution.... The organization took as its symbol a burning cross and held rallies, parades and marches around the country.*

> *....The civil rights movement of the 1960s saw a surge of local Klan activity across the South, including the bombings, beatings and shootings of black and white activists. These actions, carried out in secret but apparently the work of local Klansmen, outraged the nation and helped win support for the civil rights cause.*

> *In 1965, President Lyndon Johnson delivered a speech publicly condemning the Klan and announcing the arrest of four Klansmen in connection with the murder of a white female civil rights worker in Alabama. The cases of Klan-related violence became more isolated in the decades to come, though fragmented groups of Klansmen became aligned with neo-Nazi or other right-wing extremist organizations from the 1970s onward. In the early 1990s, the Klan was estimated to have between 6,000 and 10,000 active members, mostly in the Deep South.*[4]

The new Klan no longer burns crosses or wears pointed white hoods. They have adapted to keep up with changes in society. To view the best example of what a traditional Klansmen might look like today, turn your television to any station that talks politics. Then take a close look at some of the people who endorse the 2016 Presidential candidate, Donald Trump. If you follow politics, you have heard Donald Trump's message and you have seen the blatant racism that occurs during his rallies.

There were two incidents that occurred at his rally that made me feel like I was watching a watered-down version of the hate and racism that occurred in 1920.

One incident occurred when a Muslim man and his wife were peacefully protesting against Donald Trump at one of his rallies. They both received hostile aggression from the crowd but they remained calm.

This was America and they knew they had the right to have their own political view and that they could openly express that view anywhere. This was a miscalculation and apparently not true at a Trump rally because one white man who was a Trump follower called the Muslim man's wife a bitch and then aggressively approached the Muslim man and spit in his face. After this verbal and physical attack I expected the Muslim man to try to harm his attacker but instead he remained calm, grabbed his wife's hand, turned and exited the rally. I think he and his wife realized how much danger they were in and that their rights as U.S. citizens meant nothing in that moment.

There was a second incident that occurred at a Trump rally where adult white men intimidated and assaulted a teenage black girl. Like the Muslim man and his wife, she also attended to express her opposition to Trump's run for President and the racism expressed in his campaign. While she was walking through the crowd, she was deliberately pushed, bumped and yelled at by several hostile people. As I watched her walk through the hate filled crowd my mind flashed back to the four black college students known as the Greensboro four who received similar treatment when they participated in a peaceful sit-in at a "Whites only" lunch counter at a Woolworth's store in 1960.

The Greensboro sit-ins were a series of nonviolent protests in Greensboro, North Carolina, in 1960, which led to the Woolworth department store chain removing its policy of racial segregation in the Southern United States. While not the first sit-in of the Civil Rights Movement, the Greensboro sit-ins were an instrumental action, and also the most well-known sit-ins of the Civil Rights Movement. These sit-ins led to increased national sentiment at a crucial period in US history. The primary event took place at the Greensboro, North Carolina, Woolworth store. [5]

The Greensboro sit-in was 56 years ago. By now one would have thought that we would have addressed our differences and learned how to treat each other with respect, but apparently this is not the case.

As the adult white men with hate in their eyes bullied the little black teenage girl through the crowd;

I was **disturbed** as a human being that our society has learned nothing from the great spiritual and civil rights leaders like Gandhi, Dalai Lama, and Martin Luther King. They tried to teach us patience, peace and tolerance. It is clear that we have not listened.

I was **disappointed** to be an American citizen that lives in a country that still resorts to violence when an individual has a different view on an issue or a difference of opinion.

I was **angry** as a black man who had to watch racists bully another black person.

I was **ashamed** as a man that adult men would bully a defenseless little girl.

The men that participated in this shameless act have the same mentality as the police officers that I mentioned earlier who are damaging the public image of good police officers. We know this type of thinking and culture exists and we need to exterminate it from society. The Mayor and Police Commissioner from every city in the U.S. need to join forces to find a way to bring respect and dignity back to the blue uniform. One way to help do this might be to execute a departmental sweep to eliminate officers that have their own hidden agenda and believe that they are above the law.

TEFLON DON THEORY

The third and final reason why police brutality exists is the Teflon Don Theory. The principle of this theory tells us that in the eyes of the law, some police feel that they are untouchable. They are in denial that a structure, a code, and laws exist that they must follow in order to do their job properly.

The result of this denial is that they are reckless with the power they have been given and reckless with the lives of the people they are sworn to protect. The police that carelessly do their job; quickly learn that there are usually no consequences to their actions. They are untouchable because of the legislative infrastructure in place that is staffed with lawyers, judges, and an entire police force willing to fight for them—even when their actions result in the death of a US citizen. Tragically, this even applies when a child, an elderly person, and mentally challenged individuals, are hurt or killed.

Most would agree that police officers must have some latitude to do their job. In-fact this is pretty much required because being objective and able to use their own sensibilities is a large part of their job. As police enforce the law, they should rationally justify each action and decision. When they do, lives are saved, criminals are arrested and the good people are protected. When they don't, police officers must be held accountable.

> *Justice and freedom are meaningless words when police officers are allowed to break the very laws that they have been sworn to enforce.*

There is documented history that gives us an idea of how the Teflon Don Theory manifested. Going back only one generation, racial injustice and murder were rampant through our society. Let's analyze one such case. As you read this horrific instance of injustice and murder that occurred 86 years ago, pay close attention to similarities in our society today.

In 1930, two young African-American men, Thomas Shipp and Abram Smith, had been arrested and charged with the armed robbery and murder of a white factory worker, Claude Deeter, and the rape of his companion, a white girl named Mary Ball. A day later, local police were unable to stop a mob of thousands who broke into the jail with sledgehammers and crowbars from pulling the young men out of their cells to lynch them. [6]

Lawrence Beitler took this iconic photograph on August 7, 1930.

This disturbing picture shows us just how barbaric some people in our society can be. The two men appear to have been beaten and then they were hung without getting due process to prove their guilt or innocence of the crimes that they were charged with. In the picture you can see teenagers in the audience. They were the next generation at that time. They are going to be bringing the thinking, racism, hate and death that this crime embodies with them as they become adults. You can notice that some people appear to be smiling as if they were at a festive event or picnic. Everyone appears to have gotten dressed for the occasion as you notice the women in nice dresses and one has on what appears to be a fur coat. The men have on dress shirts and slacks.

There is one Adolf Hitler looking man who is pointing at the hanging bodies and is looking directly at the camera as if to say "You see that. You're next!"

This had to be terrifying for any black person who resided in that area at the time.

Let's assume that the men did commit the indicated crimes and that they were career criminals of the worst kind, is this justification for them to be forcibly removed from jail so that an angry mob can administer their own form of justice?

If we also assume that breaking someone out of jail is a crime, why is it that there was enough time for the mob to beat, murder, celebrate and take a picture to immortalize the event? Where were the police who were supposed to protect the victims? There is no documented proof of whether anyone in the mob was prosecuted, but law enforcement could not use the excuse that they did not know who was involved. Bystanders and perpetrators both are looking directly into the lens of the camera that took the historic picture.

This unimaginable crime happened less than a century ago. It resulted in the death of black men, there was a person taking pictures, there were witnesses of the crime, the guilt or innocence of the victims had not been decided, there was an angry mob who broke the law and decided how to prosecute them.

The circumstances of the crime left a bunch of unknown answers and the smell of conspiracy. Because of the crime there was a group of people in fear of their lives and criminals who were responsible for the murder going scot-free. How is this different from today? Looking back at black people who were killed by law enforcement in the past four years –there is no difference.

REMEMBER ME

Kimani Gray 16

New York, NY

Killed: March 9, 2013

Crime: Police said Gray pointed a revolver at them as they attempted to question him. Friends and family say Gray had never had a gun.

Aftermath: No indictments for the cops responsible for shooting Gray.

KIMANI IS WHY BLACK LIVES NEED TO MATTER

1930 AGAIN

Today, young black males still live in fear and police are not prosecuted for the commision of a crime. One incident that confirms this, occurred in May 2012 and involved 19-year-old football star named Kendrec McDade. Mr. McDade was a California college student who police fatally shot to death because of a false claim that he stole a backpack and had a gun. The truth was that Kendrec McDade had nothing to do with the theft. He was unarmed, afraid and running from police when he was killed. When the autopsy report was finally released, it revealed that Mr. McDade was shot seven times at close range and handcuffed afterward.

Cell phone store worker Oscar Carrillo lied to authorities that the two men who stole his backpack were armed. Officers Matthew Griffin and Jeffery Newlen came to the scene....they began pursuing McDade who was on foot. Reportedly, when the student allegedly reached for his waistband, one of the officers, who was in his patrol car, fired four rounds at McDade. The second officer, who was on foot, fired yet another four rounds because he "believed his partner was involved in a firefight."

Both Newlen and Griffin went on record, stating that they realized McDade was unarmed after they had already shot him. Even more upsetting, the coroner was able to determine that McDade was handcuffed after the shooting.

Pasadena police Lt. Phlunte Riddle, quickly defended the officers' actions of handcuffing the teen after he had already been shot. "Procedurally, until an individual has been deemed to be no further threat, the officer can use discretion to unhandcuff," said Lt. Riddle.

When the paramedics reportedly got to the scene, McDade was still conscious, even though he had been shot several times and remained handcuffed in his condition. During this time, McDade was called "combative,"in the police report. McDade died of his injuries at Huntington Memorial Hospital 90 minutes later.

According to Pasadena Police Chief Philip Sanchez, the erroneous chain of events and tragic end result was ignited by that phony phone call and accounts for the mindset of the officers, who wound up killing 19-year-old Kendrec McDade because they thought he was armed with a gun.

Carrillo allegedly lied about the robbery because he thought it would encourage a speedier response. It worked. Investigators fled to the scene and murdered McDade.

The police department and Los Angeles County District Attorney's Office cleared the officers of wrongdoing. Investigations by the FBI and Office of Independent Review are pending.[7]

Injustice comparison from 1930 and 2012

1930 Thomas Shipp and Abram Smith	82 years later	2012 Kendrec McDade
Accused of a crime	No difference	Accused of a crime
Was not protected by those sworn to protect civilians	No difference	Was not protected by those sworn to protect civilians
Murdered in public	No difference	Murdered in public
Not convicted in court of law	No difference	Not convicted in court of law
May have been innocent of the charges	Slight difference	Was innocent of the charges
The individuals that committed this crime may not have been held responsible	Slight difference	The individuals that committed this crime were acquitted by the District Attorney's office and were not held responsible

Both of these incidents are Teflon Don Theory cases because black men were killed, they were denied due process of the law, and no one was held responsible. It does not matter if they were killed by a police officer, night watchman, security guard, or citizen. However, in cases where police officers are involved, the collusion between District Attorney's, Lawyers, and Judges allow police to go untouched, regardless of how police do their job.

If you don't believe that there is a biased relationship between police and key court administrators, and you are not convinced that this relationship helps police manipulate the outcome of a prosecution, familiarize yourself with the story—Making a Murderer. This is a true story that was filmed over a ten year period.

It is the story of a DNA exoneree who, while exposing police corruption, becomes a suspect in a grisly new crime because of retribution by the police department he was suing for false imprisonment. [8]

The special thing about Making a Murderer is that the suspect is a man who lived in a small town who was hated by local police. He has limited formal education but proceeds through life on his own common-sense. He is also white! The story gives a vivid glimpse into just how real the Teflon Don Theory is. It touches upon police corruption, it shows how close the relationship is between criminal enforcement and criminal prosecution, and it will open your eyes to just how powerful and dangerous a law enforcement organization can be in order to support its own corruption.

Whether you believe the Retribution Theory, the Invisible Empire Theory or the Teflon Don Theory is not important. What is important is that you do not deny that we have an epidemic of epic proportion. Black people are being killed at an astronomical rate at the hands of the police for mostly misdemeanors and most times the victims are innocent. To deny that this is happening is criminal itself. We all need to come to grips and admit that this is a problem. This is the first step to solving the issue and is similar to the first thing an alcoholic must do in AA counseling. Without recognizing there is a problem and without admitting it, an alcoholic will fail the recovery program.

Denial that we even have issues with police brutality and racism is the reason why the relationship between police and black people has not gotten better. There are still very influential men like Talk radio host Rush Limbaugh, Former Mayor Rudy Guiliani and Political Commentator Bill O'Reilly who believe that all things are equal between black and white relationships with police.

Rush Limbaugh has gone so far as to call the current issues between black people and police a Democratic ploy and a myth.

> Conservative radio host Rush Limbaugh called the narrative of white cops preying on black children nationwide "a myth," claiming killings like the one in Ferguson, Mo. are "rare" but get coverage because they "further the Democratic Party's agenda."

> "So many myths are on display each and every day in this country," Limbaugh began, discussing the ongoing riots over the killing of 18-year-old Michael Brown by a police officer. "So many myths. And the myths are what make up the daily drive-by news agenda, and that is the daily news agenda of the Democratic Party."

> "The myth that is driving what happened in St. Louis is that white cops shoot black kids all the time," he said. "That is the myth, that is the image being created, that is the purpose of all the coverage."

> "It is rare — the truth of the matter is, it is rare," the radio host asserted. "The simple fact of the matter is that the greatest incidents — the most largest number of criminal incidents against blacks are perpetrated by blacks. The fact that this is rare is why it's on television." [9]

The Loch Ness monster was a myth because it could not be proven to be true. The death of black civilians is easily verified. We have cell phone video footage, we have body cam video, we have dash cam video footage, and we have families mourning the death of a loved one on the evening news. No, this is not a myth. It is a fact! One that has been happening way too much in the past few years.

Limbaugh and Guiliani conclude that black people should be more concerned about being killed by their own kind, not police.

Limbaugh stated that *"The simple fact of the matter is that the greatest incidents — the most largest number of criminal incidents against blacks are perpetrated by blacks."*

Guiliani stated that *"Ninety-three percent of blacks are killed by other blacks," ... on NBC's "Meet the Press." "I would like to see the attention paid to that instead of how police do their job."*

Even if Guiliani and Limbaugh were both correct, black on black crime is a different problem that is so far removed from the main issue that it is meaningless to mention. The issue is not about how many black people are being killed by black people, the issue is how many black people are being killed by individuals who have been sworn to protect and serve the public.

Citizens being killed by each other will always happen. No race, color, or creed can escape this reality. *Most murder in the United States is intra-racial, according to data from the Justice Department: White people are more likely to kill white people, and black people are more likely to kill black people.*

> *Nearly 84 percent of white victims from 1980 to 2008 were killed by white assailants, the department's numbers show. During the same period, 93 percent of black victims were murdered by someone of the same race.* [10]

Like Limbaugh, Bill O'Reilly has also denied that a problem between cops and blacks exists. According to O'Reilly, the statistics show that the rate at which black citizens are being killed has actually decreased.

> *"Let's take a good look at this plague of white cops acting violently against blacks, as professor Michael Eric Dyson puts it," O'Reilly said on his Dec. 1, 2014, Fox News program.*

> *"In the past 50 years, the rate of black Americans killed by police has dropped 70 percent. In 2012, 123 African-Americans were shot dead by police. There are currently more than 43 million blacks living in the U.S.A. Same year, 326 whites were killed by police bullets. Those are the latest stats available."*

> *"That's not an epidemic. It's not crazy. It's not a hunting-down of black youth."* [11]

Let's again assume that the facts O'Reilly has presented are true and that the rate at which blacks are killed has reduced over the years. Is this what the discussion is really about right now? Aren't we talking about the latest wave of very questionable killings like Eric Garner, Sandra Bland and Freddie Gray? How does pointing out a reduction in deaths help us to understand why Garner, Bland and Gray are dead? Also, I would like to know how O'Reilly was able to get accurate data on this situation? Would every instance where black people were murdered or subjected to racism really be accurately reported and put in a database? The last thing to point out with the O'Reilly claim is that basic mathematics shows that 126 black deaths is worse than the 326 white deaths because the population of blacks in America is somewhere around 6 times less. Regardless of this fact, raw numbers don't really matter and they are not needed in order to see the problem that is right in front of our faces.

By doing a simple experiment, Jane Elliot, a white American female Anti-racism activist, LGBT activist and Educator , was able to make individuals face their own denial of racial issues in America. The experiment, which was video recorded in an auditorium of close to 800 people, began with Ms. Elliot giving one instruction.

> *"I want every white person in this room, who would be happy, to be treated, as this society in general, treats our black citizens—if you as a white person would be happy to receive the same treatment that our black citizens do in this society, please stand."*

No one in the audience moved. Everyone stayed seated. Ms. Elliot continued. *"You didn't understand the directions. If you white folks want to be treated the way blacks are in this society, stand."*

Again, her instructions fell upon deaf ears. No one moved. A camera pan of the audience showed bewildered, perplexed looks on most faces. She continued.

> *"Nobody is standing here. That says very plainly that you know what's happening, you know you don't want it for you. I want to know why you are so willing to accept it or allow it to happen for others."* [12]

I wonder if Limbaugh, Juliani and O'Reilly were in the room if they would have stood up. Based on the arguments they have made, I could only conclude that they would have.

What these gentlemen are somehow missing is the fact that a high number of U.S. citizens are being killed over toy guns, broken tail lights and false reports of being a threat to others. We are all in big trouble as U.S. citizens if two influential political analysts and a man who was once the Mayor of New York City and the head of law enforcement won't acknowledge that there is a racial problem between black people and police.

There should be no doubt that we have a problem after all the murder, death, and video footage that we have watched; that our kids have seen, and that the world has witnessed.

REMEMBER ME

Eric Harris, 44

Tulsa OK

Killed; April 2, 2015

Crime: Officer confused his Taser with his Revolver and shot Harris in the back as Harris lay on the ground subdued.

Aftermath: Reserve Officer Bates was found guilty of manslaughter and sentenced to four years in prison.

ERIC IS WHY BLACK LIVES NEED TO MATTER

2

OMEGA THEORY

"I'm not going to take a chance ever in life of losing everything I worked for for 30 years because some fucking ni**er heard us say 'Ni**er' and turned us into the Enquirer magazine."[13]

- Duane "Dog" Chapman
Hollywood Actor

All throughout American history, black people were labeled as evil and disliked throughout the United States. Society was made to believe that black people were not very intelligent, that they used up resources without contributing, that they were a burden to civilization and only had value when they were sold as chattel. Over the years they were whipped, spit-on, beat, kicked and hit with night sticks. Their families were torn apart, their dignity was taken, they were treated less than civilized, then they were told to forget about it and get over it, less than a century later.

Many blacks repressed this reprehensible abuse, but most never forgot. In the 1960's a new wave of black consciousness emerged. It was at this juncture where a slight shift in the social status of black people began to occur. Society was challenged. Black people demanded equal acceptance in society. The black culture began to educate themselves on what it really meant to have an equal status in society and set goals to achieve change. A change that symbolically represented the sentiments of a song titled The revolution will not be televised from the Gil Scott Heron classic album—Pieces of a Man. The message Mr. Heron delivered in this song unfolded in society in many different ways. The black culture began to show the public that they too are worthy of dignity and respect, and that they possessed knowledge that was valuable to the survival of our civilization. While this was all occurring, the police were delivering injustice that perfectly matched Heron's 'The revolution will not be televised' message.

In dark cold places, when camera phones did not exist, police administered their own form of street justice. There were many uncorroborated charges made by victims that went uninvestigated because abuse could not be substantiated. The beatings and injustice continued for decades and no one cared. No one checked into the claims—No one gave a damn!

Reflecting upon the historical treatment of black people reminded me of a National Geographic story that I had watched about wolf packs and members of the pack called Omega wolves. The narrative caught my attention because of how closely the pack's treatment of the Omega wolves resembled society's treatment of black people.

You most likely have heard of the Alpha male and Alpha female wolves. They are the highest ranking wolves in the structure of the pack. They lead the pack, enforce pack rules, pass on survival techniques, help the pack sustain, are allowed to mate, and they eat first when a kill is made. The Omega wolves are at the absolute bottom of the hierarchy. Like the Alpha wolves, there are two Omega wolves—a male and a female. They are both punching bags for the entire wolf pack. When male wolves need to relieve aggression, or just feel like bullying another wolf, they seek out the male Omega wolf and beat him up. Female wolves in the pack do the same to the female Omega wolf. They can do this because the Omega wolves do not fight back. They always submit and take the beating that is coming. Omega wolves are not allowed to mate and they eat last when a kill is made. Ironically the Alpha wolves and Omega wolves which are both at opposite ends of the wolf pack hierarchy represent the same importance to the pack. Without either, the wolf pack may cease to exist! It is self-explanatory why the wolf pack will face extinction without Alpha wolves, but why is this true with the Omega wolves? Aggressive behavior comes with being a wolf. If every wolf in the pack is willing to fight to establish dominance and move to the next hierarchical level, the wolves within the wolf pack would kill each other. This is where the Omega wolves come in and save the day. You could say they are taking one for the team so that the wolf pack can survive.

In society, police are the Alpha wolves. They carry guns, have the legal right to kill and have the courts and legal system on their side. The Omega wolves are the people who unjustifiably get killed. In 2014 a rash of Omega wolf killings was initiated and several black people were killed; one after the other, over a period of two years.

Next Death	Name	Date Killed
	Eric Garner, 43	July 17, 2014
1 month	Michael Brown, 18	August 9, 2014
3 months	Tamir Rice, 12	Nov. 22, 2014
5 months	Freddie Gray, 25	April 19, 2015
3 months	Sandra Bland, 28	July 13, 2015
12 months	Alton Sterling, 37	July 5, 2016
1 day later	Philando Castile, 32	July 6, 2016

In each case listed above, with the exception of Michael Brown, the victim was either clearly murdered on video or the murder was covered up and defended by the officer's police department, the district attorney and justice system. We have recapped the details in each case.

REMEMBER ME

Eric Garner 43

New York, NY

Killed: July 17, 2014

Crime: Selling untaxed cigarettes

Aftermath: The New York City medical examiner ruled Mr. Garner's death a homicide. The officer involved was not indicted.

ERIC IS WHY BLACK LIVES NEED TO MATTER

Photo Courtesy of Yahoo!

Eric Garner was killed by officer Daniel Pantaleo who restrained Mr. Garner with a prohibited NYPD chokehold. Mr. Garner was killed on July 17, 2014 in Tompkinsville, Staten Island shortly after he had broken up a fight. Mr. Garner's death was recorded on video by Ramsey Orta who was a friend of Mr. Garner.

Eric Garner was a 6ft 3in tall, 350-pound, 43-year-old African American man. He was approached by Justin Damico, a plainclothes police officer who accused Mr. Garner of selling loose cigarettes, which is in violation of New York state law. Mr. Garner's side of the dialogue with officer Damico was captured along with video footage.

> *Mr. Garner: "Get away...for what? Every time you see me, you want to mess with me. I'm tired of it. It stops today. Why would you? Everyone standing here will tell you I didn't do nothing. I did not sell nothing. Because every time you see me, you want to harass me. You want to stop me from selling cigarettes. I'm minding my business, officer, I'm minding my business. Please just leave me alone. I told you the last time, please just leave me alone."*

> *As Mr. Garner and officer Damico were in a verbal exchange, officer Pantaleo approached Mr. Garner from behind and attempted to handcuff him, Mr. Garner swatted his arms away, saying "Don't touch me, please."* [14]

This is when officer Pantaleo put Mr. Garner in the chokehold that is prohibited by NYPD regulations. With the chokehold firmly applied officer Pantaleo pulled the 6ft 3in tall, 350-pound Mr. Garner to the ground.

Mr. Garner fell to his knees and forearms with the weight of officer Pantaleo on his back with the chokehold applied and was unable to speak. A few seconds later officer Pantaleo released the chokehold and pushed Mr. Garner's face into the sidewalk.

Bystanders heard Mr. Garner say "I can't breathe" eleven times! as officer Pantaleo pushed Mr. Garner's face into the sidewalk. Shortly after his plea for air, Mr. Garner passed out and was motionless and handcuffed on the sidewalk for several minutes. When the ambulance arrived on scene, two medics and two EMTs inside the ambulance were slow to administer any emergency medical aid. According to police, Mr. Garner had a heart attack while being transported to Richmond University Medical Center. He was pronounced dead at the hospital one hour later.

One of the NYPD officers at the scene of the murder was officer Kizzy Adoni, a female African American NYPD sergeant. When asked why she or none of the other officers tried to assist Mr. Garner with his breathing, she replied that "The perpetrator's condition did not seem serious and he did not appear to get worse." Other officers stated that they did not start CPR because Mr. Garner was still breathing and it would have been improper to do CPR on someone who was breathing on his own.

Mr. Garner was described by his friends as a "neighborhood peacemaker" and as a generous, congenial person. He was the father of six children and had three grandchildren. At the time of his death Mr. Garner's youngest child was three months old. [14]

One Month Later

Michael Brown

Was Killed

REMEMBER ME

Michael Brown 18

Ferguson MO

Killed: Aug 9, 2014

Crime: Fighting with a police officer

Aftermath: The officer was not indicted by a grand jury. He subsequently resigned from the Ferguson police force.

MICHAEL IS WHY BLACK LIVES NEED TO MATTER

Michael Brown, a 18 year-old African American teen was killed on August 9, 2014 by Officer Darren Wilson when he stopped Mr. Brown and a friend who were under suspicion of a convenience store robbery. Early accounts for how Mr. Brown was killed came from Officer Wilson and witnesses who were in the area at the time of the incident. The information provided by the two sources varied drastically. For example, Officer Wilson described Mr. Brown's demeanor as a menacing, aggressive individual. Witnesses on the scene and residents who knew Mr. Brown, described him as a fun-loving kid who had just graduated from high school. They also told authorities that Mr. Brown was set to start Community College just days after he was killed. This drastic variation of the facts also existed when each side gave their account of how and why Michael Brown was killed. Because of these inconsistencies, we will use the details reported by the Department of Justice and the Attorney General who did an independent investigation to describe the incident.

Police dispatch received a call reporting the theft of several packs of cigarillos from the Ferguson Market and Liquor store. The 6' 5", 289lb eighteen year-old had allegedly bullied the store attendant and took them by force. Officer Wilson was in the area on patrol when the call came in and he was given a description of the suspects. As he patrolled the area he noticed Mr. Brown and another teen who matched the suspect description walking in the street away from the direction of the convenience store. Upon closer observation Officer Wilson noticed that Mr. Brown was holding cigarillos in his hand.

According to the Department of Justice report, Officer Wilson pulled his SUV police vehicle in front of Mr. Brown and the other teen to block their way and attempted to exit his vehicle.

As he opened the door it made contact with Mr. Brown. Mr. Brown pushed the door closed, forcing Officer Wilson back into his SUV and punched Officer Wilson in the jaw.

This is corroborated by bruising on Wilson's jaw, scratches on his neck and the presence of Mr. Brown's DNA on Wilson's collar, shirt, and pants...[15]

A struggle ensued. Officer Wilson stated that he reached for his gun to protect himself because his position in the SUV restricted access to less lethal weapons. Mr. Brown also went after the gun. During the struggle Officer Wilson's was able to gain enough control to fire the gun. The discharged bullet struck Mr. Brown in the hand.

Autopsy results, skin from Mr. Brown's palm on the outside of the SUV, bullet trajectory, as well as Mr. Brown's DNA on the inside of the driver's door, corroborate Wilson's account...[15]

After being struck by the bullet, Mr. Brown retreated and started to run away from the SUV.

Mr. Brown ran at least 180 feet away from the SUV, as verified by the location of bloodstains on the roadway, which DNA analysis confirmed as Mr. Brown's blood.[15]

No shots were fired during Mr. Brown's retreat. At some point Mr. Brown turned around and headed back in Officer Wilson's direction where he met gunfire.

The autopsy results confirm that Wilson did not shoot Mr. Brown in the back as he was running away because there were no entrance wounds to Mr. Brown's back.[15]

Officer Wilson shot twelve bullets at Mr. Brown, striking him eight times as Mr. Brown fell to his death. Wilson stated that he shot Mr. Brown because he feared for his safety as Mr. Brown charged at him.

Wilson fired at Mr. Brown in what appeared to be self-defense and stopped firing once Mr. Brown fell to the ground. Wilson stated that he feared Mr. Brown would again assault him because of Mr. Brown's conduct at the SUV...[15]

Mr. Brown was found dead on the ground with his injured hand by his side and his other hand balled in a fist. Investigators were unable to establish whether there was any time before Mr. Brown was killed if he had his hands in the air and tried to surrender.

Although there are several individuals who have stated that Mr. Brown held his hands up in an unambiguous sign of surrender prior to Wilson shooting him dead, their accounts do not support a prosecution of Wilson... Some of those accounts are inaccurate because they are inconsistent with the physical and forensic evidence; Certain other witnesses who originally

stated Mr. Brown had his hands up in surrender recanted their original accounts, admitting that they did not witness the shooting...despite what they initially reported either to federal or local law enforcement or to the media. The U.S. Department of Justice concluded that Wilson shot Mr. Brown in self-defense. [16]

Three Months Later
Tamir Rice
Was Killed

REMEMBER ME

Tamir Rice 12

Cleveland OH

Killed: Nov. 22, 2014

Crime: Playing in a park with a BB gun

Aftermath: Mr. Rice's family has filed a wrongful death lawsuit against Cleveland.

TAMIR IS WHY BLACK LIVES NEED TO MATTER

Tamir Rice, a 12 year-old African American youth was killed by Officer Timothy Loehmann on November 22, 2014, in Cleveland, Ohio. Mr. Rice was shot dead when Officer Loehmann and his partner Officer Frank Garmback responded to a dispatch call regarding a person in a park with a gun.

Tamir Rice was playing with a BB gun across the street from a recreation center. Unsure whether the gun was fake, people in the recreation center made a precautionary call to the police so they could look into it. Officer Loehmann and Officer Garmback were in the area so they were dispatched to investigate the call. As they headed toward the park, they only knew that someone had a gun. No other information was available at the time. According to authorities, subsequent calls had come in to report that it was possible that the gun was fake and that the person who had it was a teenager. Unfortunately, this information did not reach the officer's in time. Once on the scene, the patrol car pulled into the park adjacent to where Mr. Rice was playing and Officer Loehmann immediately fired two shots. One of the shots hit Mr. Rice in the chest and he fell to the ground. Mr. Rice died a day later from his injuries.

A deep investigation into Mr. Rice's death concluded that when the police car pulled adjacent to him in the park that he had the toy gun holstered between his belt and body. As the patrol car was stopping alongside him, he pulled the gun out to either show it or give it to the officers and he was immediately shot.

The officers reported that upon their arrival, Mr. Rice reached towards a gun in his waistband. Within two seconds of arriving on the scene, Loehmann fired two shots hitting Mr. Rice once in the torso. [17]

The investigation also determined that the police chief communicated that Officer Loehmann warned Mr. Rice three times to show his hands before he fired his weapon and Mr. Rice did not comply. This statement changed once the video evidence was released that showed a rapidly accelerated event; one so quick, that Officer Loehmann did not have time to shout a warning to Mr. Rice.

In fact, Mr. Rice was shot before the police car rolled to a stop.

> *According to Judge Ronald B. Adrine in a judgement entry on the case "this court is still thunderstruck by how quickly this event turned deadly.... On the video the ..car containing Patrol Officers Loehmann and Garmback is still in the process of stopping when Mr. Rice is shot."* [17]

Other details that emerged from the shooting noted that Officer Loehmann had previously been deemed as unfit to be a policeman while working for a different department.

> *In a memo written to the human resources manager in the city of Independence where officer Loehmann once worked, Deputy police chief Jim Polak stated that Loehmann had resigned from his unit instead of being terminated due to concerns that he lacked the emotional stability to be a police officer. Polak said that Loehmann was unable to follow "basic functions as instructed". He specifically cited a "dangerous loss of composure" that occurred in a weapons training exercise, during which Loehmann's weapons handling was "dismal" and he became visibly "distracted and weepy" as a result of relationship problems. The memo concluded, "Individually, these events would not be considered major situations, but when taken together they show a pattern of a lack of maturity, indiscretion and not following instructions, I do not believe time, nor training, will be able to change or correct these deficiencies." It was subsequently revealed that Cleveland police officials never reviewed Loehmann's personnel file from the Independence police department prior to hiring him.* [17]

Sadly, the investigation revealed that police had no compassion for Mr. Rice's mother and sister as they rushed to the scene to find out what had happened. Mr. Rice's mother who was understandably in hysteria, feverishly ran towards Mr. Rice while he was on the ground until she was stopped by police who threatened to arrest her if she did not get control of herself after they told her about her son's shooting. Mr. Rice's 14-year old sister who was also in a panic after hearing about her brother was handcuffed by police and forced to sit in a patrol car until she calmed down.

> *Mr. Rice's mother said that ... police threatened her with arrest if she did not calm down after being told about her son's shooting.* [17]

> *A second video shows Mr. Rice's 14-year-old sister being forced to the ground, handcuffed and placed in a patrol car after she ran toward her brother about two minutes after the shooting.* [17]

The District Attorney summarized the tragedy as a series of misfortunate mistakes that all contributed to Mr. Rice's death – including Mr. Rice. Because of this, the officers involved should not be prosecuted.

> *The District Attorney stated.... "Given this perfect storm of human error, mistakes, and communications by all involved that day, the evidence did not indicate criminal conduct by police."*

> *On December 28, 2015, Grand Jury returned their decision declining to indict the police officers.*

> *On April 25, 2016, the lawsuit was settled, with the City of Cleveland in the amount of $6 million.*

> *Mr. Rice was remembered "for his budding talents and described as a popular child who liked to draw, play basketball and perform in the school's drumline."* [17]

Five Months Later

Freddie Gray

was killed

REMEMBER ME

Freddie Gray 25

Baltimore MD

Killed: April 19, 2015

Crime: Being in the wrong place at the wrong time.

Aftermath: City of Baltimore reached a $6.4 million settlement with Mr. Gray's family.

FREDDIE IS WHY BLACK LIVES NEED TO MATTER

Freddie Gray, a 25 year-old African American man was killed when injuries he received between the time he was arrested and the time he arrived at the West Baltimore police station caused him to fall into a coma. He died a few days later in the hospital due to his injuries.

Mr. Gray was in an area in Baltimore that was littered with abandon homes and was known to harbor drug activity. Mr. Gray was loitering in the area when he spotted police on bike patrol in the area. Once Mr. Gray noticed that the police saw him he began to run and the police gave chase. Once he was apprehended, police noticed that Mr. Gray was carrying a switchblade type of knife that they believed was illegal. However, they later found out that the knife was legal under Maryland state law.

According to the state's attorney for Baltimore City, the spring-assisted knife Mr. Gray was carrying was legal under Maryland law....[18]

Witnesses reported that Mr. Gray was beaten by several police with batons, that he was held down with his limbs bent in unnatural positions and that he was kneed in the neck with the full weight of an adult male behind the impact. Once the "rough-housing" was done, witnesses said that Mr. Gray was dragged into a police transport van and it looked as though he was unable to fully use his legs to get into the van.

Six days before Mr. Gray was arrested a new policy of making sure handcuffed individuals in transport were properly secured with a seatbelt, was issued.

The policy was implemented in order to prevent injuries during transport. This policy was not followed when Mr. Gray was transported. Speculation is that in addition to the rough-house beating that Mr. Gray took outside the van, that he was subjected to what is known as a "Rough Ride." This occurs when the driver of the transport vehicle drives in a manner to purposefully cause passengers to get slammed around in the steel cabin of the transport van. Once the "Rough Ride" was over and police realized the seriousness of Mr. Gray's condition, they brought him to the trauma center. Mr. Gray lasted almost a week in a coma until he died of his injuries.

> ... *Mr. Gray suffered from total cardiopulmonary arrest at least once at the trauma center but was resuscitated without ever regaining consciousness. He remained in a coma, and underwent extensive surgery in an effort to save his life. Mr. Gray's family reported that the doctor told them that he had three fractured vertebrae, injuries to his voice box, and his spine was 80% severed at his neck... Mr. Gray died on April 19, 2015, a week after his arrest.* [18]

The medical examination of Mr. Gray's body determined that the injuries he sustained were a result of the "Rough Ride" he received and the prosecutor deemed Mr. Gray's death a homicide. Six officers, three white and three black were charge with Mr. Gray's death.

Details of Charges for Freddie Gray Death

Officer William G. Porter	Charged with involuntary manslaughter; second degree assault; misconduct in office	All charges dismissed
Officer Caesar R. Goodson, Jr.	Charged with second-degree depraved heart murder; involuntary manslaughter; second-degree assault; manslaughter by vehicle (gross negligence); manslaughter by vehicle (criminal negligence); misconduct in office and reckless endangerment.	Found not guilty on all charges
Officer Garrett E. Miller	Two counts of second degree assault; two counts of misconduct in office; and false imprisonment.	Charges dropped at pretrial hearing
Officer Edward M. Nero	Two counts of second degree assault; misconduct in office and false imprisonment.	Found not guilty on all charges
Lt. Brian W. Rice	He was charged with involuntary manslaughter; two counts of second degree assault; manslaughter by vehicle (gross negligence); two counts of misconduct in office; and false imprisonment.	Found not guilty on all counts by Judge
Sgt. Alicia D. White	Charged with involuntary manslaughter; second degree assault; misconduct and reckless endangerment.	Charges dropped at pretrial hearing

On September 8, 2015, Baltimore Mayor Stephanie Rawlings-Blake announced that the city had reached a $6.4 million settlement with Mr. Gray's family.[18]

Three Months Later

Sandra Bland

was killed

REMEMBER ME

Sandra Bland, 28

Waller County TX

Killed: July 13, 2015

Crime: Failure to use turn signal.

Aftermath: Ms. Bland's family settled a wrongful death lawsuit for 1.9 million against Waller County. No one was charged for Ms. Bland's murder.

SANDRA IS WHY BLACK LIVES NEED TO MATTER

Sandra Bland a 28 year-old African American woman was physically assaulted during a routine traffic stop, then she was falsely arrested and subsequently found dead, hanging in her jail cell. She had multiple autopsies; however the coroner in the same county where she was jailed classified her death as a suicide.

Ms. Bland was pulled over for failure to use a turn signal during a lane change on July 10, 2015 by state trooper Brian Encinia. Initially, the interaction between Ms. Bland and Officer Encinia followed the standard traffic stop procedure. Officer Encinia pulled Ms. Bland over, explained why she was getting stopped, then went to his patrol car, wrote a traffic warning and returned to her driver's side window.

Dash cam video footage of the incident was reviewed by former NYC police officer Eugene O'Donnell and former St. Louis police officer Reddit Hudson with CNN correspondent Jake Tapper. Both officers state that at this point Officer Encinia should have handed Ms. Bland her ticket and stated that "this is a warning for failing to use your turn signal." Then he should have let her sign it and leave. Instead a confrontational dialogue occurred after the officer baited and goaded Ms. Bland. This was the point at which this minor traffic stop escalated into an unnecessary series of events that led to Ms. Bland's death.

The following is the dialogue that occurred when Officer Encinia returned from his patrol car to Ms. Bland's driver side window after writing the warning:

CAN I JUST HAVE MY TICKET?

Officer Encinia	*"You Ok?"*
Ms. Bland	*"I'm waiting on you. This is your job."*
Officer Encinia	*"You seem irritated."*

Ms. Bland	*"I am, I really am. You were tailing me so I move over and you stop me, so yes I am irritated."*
Officer Encinia	*"Are you done?"*
Ms. Bland	*"You asked me what was wrong and I told you, so yes I am done now."*
Officer Encinia	*"Put out your cigarette please."*
Ms. Bland	*"I'm in my car I don't have to put out my cigarette."*
Officer Encinia	*"Well you can step out now."*
Ms. Bland	*"I don't have to step out of my car... why do I have to step out?"*
Officer Encinia	*"Ma'am step out that car or I will remove you."*

Officer Encinia pulls Ms. Blands driver's side door open

Ms. Bland	*"I refuse to talk to you other than to identify myself.."*
Officer Encinia	*"Step out or I will remove you."*
Ms. Bland	*"I am getting removed for a failure to.."*
Officer Encinia	*"Step out or I will remove you. I am giving you a lawful order. Get out of the car now! I am going to yank you out of there.*

At this point Officer Encinia reaches into Ms. Blands car and grabs her.

Ms. Bland	*"Ok! You gonna yank me out of my car.. Ok, alright. Let's do this"*
Officer Encinia	*"We're going to."*

Officer Encinia grabs and pulls on Ms. Bland but she pulls back to prevent him from pulling her out of the car. They struggle with each other.

Ms. Bland	*"Don't touch me! I am not under arrest!"*
Officer Encinia	*"You are under arrest!"*
Ms. Bland	*"I'm under arrest for what!"*

Ms. Bland asks this question three times and does not get an answer.

Officer Encinia:	*"Get out of the car!"*

This time after Officer Encinia commands Ms. Bland to get out of the car, he removes his Taser from his belt and points it at her.

Officer Encinia	*"Get out of the car or I will light you up!"*
Ms. Bland	*"Wow! Wow! All this for a failure to signal."*
Officer Encinia:	*"Get out of the car or I will light you up!"*

Ms. Bland finally concedes and Officer Encinia makes her walk out of dash cam view. At this point Officer Encinia and Ms. Bland can no longer be seen by the dash cam.

Ms. Bland	*"You feeling good about yourself, you feeling good about yourself, don't you. All this for failure to signal."*
Officer Encinia	*"Turn around! Turn around now!"*
Ms. Bland	*"Why am I being arrested!"*
Officer Encinia	*"Turn around now!"*
Ms. Bland	*"Can you tell me why I am being arrested?!"*
Officer Encinia	*"I will tell you. I am giving you a lawful order!"*
Ms. Bland	*"I can't wait till we go to court! Ooooh I can't wait!"*

Officer Encinia tells Ms. Bland to stay still as she is lying on the ground in handcuffs, then he goes and walks around her car and begins to look in it like he is doing a search for something illegal, then he goes off camera where Ms. Bland is. Then a scuffle ensues...

Ms. Bland	*"..You are going to break my wrist!! Can you stop!!"*
Officer Encinia	*"Stop moving! Stop moving!!"*

At this point Ms. Blands starts screaming and then starts crying.

Ms. Bland	*"..Stop, stop,, owww, !!"*

Scuffling can be heard.

Officer Encinia	*"Stop Now!!!"*

Ms. Bland can be heard whimpering

At this point much of the video was censored due to the high level of profanity used by Ms. Bland as she cursed Officer Encinia for injuring her during the interaction.

In a video recorded by a bystander, Ms. Bland is lying on the ground with Officer Encinia and a female police officer above her. Ms. Bland says that she cannot hear, and states that the officer has slammed her head into the ground. In the video, Officer Encinia orders the bystander to leave the area.[19][20][21]

Once the bystander leaves the area, Officer Encinia and a second officer who arrived on the scene help Ms. Bland get into the back seat of the patrol car so she can be taken to jail.

Ms. Bland spent three days in a Waller County jail cell for assaulting a public servant. On the third day she was found hanging dead in her jail cell. The Waller County coroner ruled her death as a suicide. However, missing surveillance video evidence of Ms. Bland in her jail cell raises suspicion that Ms. Bland may have in-fact been murdered.

In January 2016, the grand jury indicted Officer Encinia for perjury. The charge resulted from his statement in an affidavit which claimed that he was removing Ms. Bland from her car "to further conduct a safe traffic investigation". According to a special prosecutor, the grand jury found that statement to be false. The Texas Department of Public Safety fired Officer Encinia as a result of his indictment.

In September 2016, Ms. Bland's family settled for $1.9 million in a wrongful death civil lawsuit.

Twelve Months Later

Alton Sterling

was killed

REMEMBER ME

Alton Sterling 37

Baton Rouge LA

Killed: July 5, 2016

Crime: Selling CD's

Aftermath: Officer Blane Salamoni and Officer Howie Lake II have been placed on administrative leave pending an investigation.

ALTON IS WHY BLACK LIVES NEED TO MATTER

Photo Courtesy of Yahoo!

Alton Sterling, a 37 year-old African American man who was known as "CD Man", was killed when he was shot at close range during a struggle with a police officer. He was reportedly trying to access a gun that he was carrying, to assault a Baton Rouge police officer during the scuffle.

Officer Salamoni and Officer Lake received notification from dispatch that an anonymous caller reported that a man in a red shirt was selling CD's in front of a convenience store and that he had threatened several people with a gun. When they arrived at the store they found Mr. Sterling, who matched the suspect's description in front of the store.

The convenience store owner Abdullah Muflahi managed to record the incident on his cell phone which he hid from police so they would not take it from him, as they did his store video recording. After the incident, Muflahi submitted the video to the local news outlet and posted it on social media.

The 1 minute video shows the officers in a conversation with Mr. Sterling, but the audio could not be heard. At one point in the video, one officer tased Mr. Sterling and rushes him. The two wrestle with each other then the other officer intervenes and helps to force Mr. Sterling to the ground. There appears to be a ground struggle and one of the officers can be heard yelling "He's got a gun! He's got a gun!...He is going for the gun!" After a few seconds three gun shots can be heard and the video goes black. This might have been because the person filming ducked out of harm's way when

the shots were heard. The video comes back in focus after the last gunshot was heard. When it refocuses, one officer is out of view, the other officer is on the ground at Mr. Sterling's head with his gun pointed at Mr. Sterling who can be seen lying flat on his back with a puddle of blood in the center of his shirt. The officer can be heard letting dispatch know that shots have been fired. Mr. Sterling who has been shot in the chest, is disoriented and still lying flat on his back. His eyes can be seen rolling to the back of his head as he tries to lift his left arm in the air above his chest. He gets his arm almost straight then it begins to shake as the video fades out.

According to the coroner who performed the autopsy Mr. Sterling died as a result of his injuries.

The video and circumstances of the Alton Sterling killing has left the public with several unanswered questions. Here are a few:

What actually was the initial charge against Mr. Sterling?

Whether or not Mr. Sterling had a gun is still under investigation; however, if we agree that he did have a gun and we know that Louisiana is a state with lax gun laws, is that reason alone enough to alarm a Louisiana police officer?

Was Mr. Sterling trying to access his gun so that he could kill the officers?

The only information available to answer the first question is that an anonymous caller stated that Mr. Sterling was threatening people with a gun. This is all that is known. No formal charges that reflect the initial reason that Mr. Sterling was questioned were ever filed.

This was the exact same thing that occurred in the Tamir Rice tragedy. How is it that a random call to report "suspicious activity" can get someone killed?

We can use the Louisiana gun laws for supporting data on the second question of whether a person with a gun in Louisiana is reason enough to alarm a police officer in Louisiana?

Like many states in the South, Louisiana possesses a casual stance towards gun laws. In comparison to other states, a prospective firearm owner in Louisiana will encounter less regulation and restriction in regards to purchasing, and registering a gun.

The Brady Campaign (a spin-off of the Brady bill, which requires background checks for all firearm sales), provides a scorecard for all 50 states based on their particular laws towards obtaining a gun license and gun permit. The higher the score, the stricter the policy and vice-versa. Out of a possible 100 points, Louisiana managed to score a 2.

When purchasing a firearm in a Louisiana gun shop, a buyer will encounter limited procedural barriers. Louisiana is commonly referred to as a "gun loving state." [22]

Now that we know that having a gun in Louisiana is common, the only information needed to resolve question two is:

Was Mr. Sterlingas a law abiding gun holder?
Did the officers have the answer to this question before approaching Mr. Sterling?

The answer to these questions will be revealed during the Department of Justice investigation.

We can use historical data and common police procedure to help evaluate the last question.

Was Mr. Sterling trying to access his gun so that he could kill the officers?

Mr. Sterling was killed shortly after an officer yelled "He's got a gun! He's got a gun!...He is going for the gun!" My research has revealed similar cases where this distress call is almost standard, even as it applies to law abiding citizens. Two examples that support this claim – the Noel Aguilar killing which happened in California and the Marcus Jeter framing attempt that occurred in New Jersey.

NOEL AGUILAR

Although many of the circumstances regarding exactly how and why Mr. Aguilar was killed still remain a mystery, what we do know is that police stopped Mr. Aguilar because he was riding his bike while wearing earbuds and that he was killed during his encounter with police.

Yes, commuting with earbuds in California is illegal.

> *Earbuds can't be worn in, on, or around one's ears, regardless of whether any audio is playing. There's one exception to this law: a driver, cyclist, or biker may have one bud in his or her ear and legally operate his or her vehicle. Failing to follow this law can result in a fine up to $160. While this may seem nitpicky, this law is in place for the safety of the cyclists.* [23]

As with Alton Sterling the ground struggle between police and Mr. Aguilar was recorded on video. The circumstances were almost identical to Mr. Sterling's.

The two officers wrestled Mr. Aguilar to the ground and there was a struggle and commotion. One officer asks "Is it a gun?!" The other responds with "It's a gun!, it's a gun!" One officer attempts to put the handcuffs on Mr. Aguilar as he struggles. The other officer has a knee on Mr. Aguilar's neck. A gunshot is heard and one of the officers screams "Ahhhhh!!! I've been shot! I've been shot! One officer shot the other officer by mistake, but they both blamed it on Mr. Aguilar who at this time is already handcuffed and on his stomach. Mr. Aguilar can be heard saying "I didn't shoot nobody! I didn't shoot nobody!" The officers are still on top of Mr. Aguilar. Moments later a singular gunshot can be heard which was followed by three more. The shots are fired at the 2:40 mark in the video where Mr. Aguilar can be heard saying "Im dying! I'm dying!" and struggles to stay alive. The officer who was shot in the stomach leaves the scene to get medical aid while the other officer remained on top of a dying Mr. Aguilar. Residents can be heard in the background telling the officer to get off of Mr. Aguilar, but the officer stays on top of him until the 6:40 mark in the video – an entire 4 minutes. As one journalist puts it, *this was done to squeeze the life out of Mr. Aguilar.* [24]

With Aguilar now handcuffed, shot and mortally wounded, the officers, for several minutes put their entire body weight on him in what could only be described as an attempt to squeeze the life out of him. It worked. By the time backup arrived, Aguilar was lifeless and would never speak another word again [24]

This is one of the clearest cases of police misconduct you'll ever see. Not only did one officer clumsily shoot the other, but they senselessly and needlessly fired their guns into the back of an handcuffed, unarmed man. [24]

According to a police statement: Mr. Aguilar was shot because he *"tried to take an officer's gun."* [24]

Today, both officers are back on duty.

MARCUS JETER

A similar incident occurred when New Jersey police charged Marcus Jeter for eluding police, resisting arrest and assault. During what he thought was a routine traffic stop, Mr. Jeter was pulled to the side of the road by a police officer that had been trailing him. In an instant two officers were at the driver's side of his car. Both had guns pointing at Mr. Jeter. One had his standard issued service revolver, the other had a shotgun. As soon as Mr. Jeter saw the guns he immediately took his hands off the steering wheel and held them up. One officer ordered Mr. Jeter to get out of the car, but he did not move. He was in shock and in fear for his life. As the officers yelled for him to get out of his car another police cruiser barreled head-on into Mr. Jeter's car while recklessly driving in the opposite direction of normal traffic flow.

The impact caused Mr. Jeter to hit his forehead on the steering wheel. After his forehead struck the steering wheel his body was abruptly returned to the upright position. At that moment, he saw the driver of the police cruiser run to the passenger side of his car. At the same time, one of the officers that was already on the scene used his baton to break the driver's side window. Glass fragments shattered into Mr. Jeter's face. While Mr. Jeter was pulling away to avoid the shattered glass, one of the officers punched him in the face and another officer unsuccessfully attempted to yank him out of his car because he was wearing his seatbelt.

When the officer noticed this, he abruptly disengaged the seatbelt while hitting Mr. Jeter in the back of the head and elbowing him in the jaw. While all of this was happening Mr. Jeter was screaming in pain, but he was careful to keep his hands in the air to prevent himself from getting shot. As the officer struck Mr. Jeter, the officer yelled *"Stop trying to take my gun! Stop resisting arrest! Stop trying to take my gun!"* [25] Once the seat belt was off, Mr. Jeter was yanked from the car and slammed onto the ground. The three officers piled on top of him and as one of them handcuffed him, another officer yelled, "Stop trying to resist arrest! Why are you resisting arrest! Why are you trying to take my gun!" Meanwhile, the third officer was hitting Mr. Jeter in the back of the head with his flashlight. One officer picked Mr. Jeter up and slammed him on the hood of the police cruiser and proceeded to give him a pat down. After finding nothing, the officer hit Mr. Jeter in the back of the head with his flashlight one more time and shoved him into the back of his police cruiser.

Mr. Jeter was facing five years in prison for charges that the DA filed. At the time charges were filed against Mr. Jeter, the District Attorney was only aware of one police dash cam video—a second one surfaced later and was admitted into evidence at the insistence of the defense attorney. Once the second dash cam video was submitted as evidence, all charges were dropped. Without the second dash cam video, Mr. Jeter would surely be in jail today.

In each incident that was just outlined, the statement "Why are you trying to take my gun!" was yelled by at least one

officer before an individual was killed or brutalized. Either minorities have a high incidence of brazenly trying to take an arresting officer's gun or this statement is a tactic that police use in order to justify police brutality. In these tragedies Mr. Sterling and Mr. Aguilar were killed and Mr. Jeter was brutalized throughout his entire ordeal.

The proposition that minorities have a high incidence of brazenly trying to take an arresting officer's weapon might be more palatable if the individuals being arrested were involved in criminal activity like selling drugs, were considered armed and dangerous, were arrested during a break in, or were arrested in the middle of an assault and battery. But this wasn't the case in any of these incidences.

Mr. Sterling was selling CD's, Mr. Aguilar was riding his bike wearing earbuds and Mr. Jeter was pulled over while driving the speed limit. If the statement "Why are you trying to take my gun!" is a tactic to justify murder, we need to find a way to stop it.

One possible solution is to use sensor technology to design guns that will only fire when held by the arresting officer. This would protect both the individual and officer and eliminate the "Why are you trying to take my gun!" phenomenon. In many instances before police kill minorities during a struggle, they can be heard, in a panicked voice, yelling." He is trying to take my gun!" With guns that have sensor design, the threat to the officer is minimized in these instances. The way this would work would be similar to how smartphones work. Smart phones have an option to unlock when reading a fingerprint. Gun sensor technology would work the same. When the officer grabs his weapon sensors would read the print of any finger touching the gun. If the fingerprint does not match the pre-programmed fingerprint ID, the gun will not fire. This technology could only be leveraged if it can be designed so that the safety and risk to the officer is not jeopardized.

One Day Later

Mr. Philando Castile

Was Killed

REMEMBER ME

Philando Castile 32

Falcon Heights MN

Killed: July 6, 2016

Crime: Reaching for license and registration

Aftermath: Officer Jeronimo Yanez was placed on paid administrative leave pending an investigation.

PHILANDO IS WHY BLACK LIVES NEED TO MATTER

Just a day after Alton Sterling was killed, Philando Castile an African American man was killed during a routine traffic stop. Mr. Castile was fatally shot when he reached to get his license and registration.

The incident started when officer Jeronimo Yanez stopped Mr. Castile and his girlfriend Diamond Reynolds in Falcon Heights Minnesota, allegedly for a broken taillight. The actual reason is still unknown because officer Yanez, claimed that the reason he made the stop was because Mr. Castile looked like a robbery suspect— a claim highly disputed during trial by one of Mr. Castile's attorney's.

> "..if Officer Yanez actually thought Mr. Castile was a robbery suspect, the police would have made a "felony traffic stop" (this involves "bringing the suspect out at gunpoint while officers are in a position of cover on the ground until they can identify the individual") rather than an ordinary traffic stop (in which officers stop the car and ask the driver to produce documents). So either, "Castile was a robbery suspect and Yanez didn't follow the procedures for a felony stop, or Castile was not a robbery suspect and Yanez shot a man because he stood at his window getting his information."[26]

Coincidentally this was not the first, second or third time Mr. Castile was pulled over for a traffic stop. It was the 53rd time over a 14 year time period. This amounts to almost 4 times a year.

> All the citations were for petty misdemeanors or misdemeanors, and he paid a total of $6,588 in fines. The charges most often dismissed were failure to wear a seat belt — along with driving without proof of insurance and driving with a revoked license. [27]

Once Mr. Castile's traffic record was reviewed in detail, lawyers, politicians and the public believed that Mr. Castile had been racially profiled over a 14 year time period.

Accounts of the traffic stop that resulted in the tragic death of Mr. Castile left more questions than answers.

When Officer Yanez approached the driver's side of the vehicle, he spoke with Mr. Castile who was the driver. (From this point the only information available regarding the incident came from Diamond Reynolds who was a passenger in the car. No officer account could be found.)

Once Officer Yanez reached the driver's side window he ordered Mr. Castile and Ms. Reynolds to put their hands in the air; they complied. Then he asked for license and registration. Mr. Castile reached to get his wallet to give the officer his license and registration and told Officer Yanez that he is carrying a firearm. Anticipating that something would go wrong Ms. Reynolds quickly yelled *"But he's licensed ....!"* Before she could finish her statement, Officer Yanez shot Mr. Castile four times while yelling "Don't move! Don't move!" At this point the quick thinking Ms. Reynolds grabbed her cell phone to make a live video of Mr. Castile as he lay slumped in the driver's seat dying. The heart wrenching video shows a red blotch of blood on the white t-shirt that Mr. Castile was wearing. It slowly grows as blood from the bullet wounds seep from Mr. Castile's body. At one point Ms. Reynolds looked directly into her cell phone and says, *"They killed my boyfriend."* Mr. Castile died in the County Medical Center, about 20 minutes after being shot.

Mr. Castile was born in St. Louis, Missouri in 1984. He graduated from Saint Paul Central High School in 2001 and worked for the Saint Paul Public School District for 14 years until his death.

Office Yanez was placed on paid administrative leave pending an investigation of Mr. Castile's death.

The stop occurred in a mostly white town of 5,000 and Minnesota Gov. Mark Dayton, in an extraordinary rebuke of police, said flatly that he believed the handling of the traffic stop was based on Castile's race. Mr. Castile's mother, Valerie Castile, told CNN that she had taught her son to be extremely cautious when encountering members of law enforcement. "If you get stopped by the police, ..."Comply, comply, comply." She also told CNN that "My son was a law-abiding citizen, and he did nothing wrong," she said. "He's no thug." She added, "I think he was just black in the wrong place."[26]

The tragic killing of Mr. Castille and the other five individuals mentioned, compared to the total number of black citizens who were killed by police officers across the country between 2012 and 2016, is miniscule. The actual number, which varies based on the source, averages somewhere between 400 and 500.. This is a little more than 100 black deaths each year. These numbers don't take into account whether the individuals apprehended were innocent or guilty of any crime.

Of the six killings outlined in this chapter, the data concludes that five out of six were victims were innocent or were at most, guilty of a minor infraction. In one case, the Michael Brown case, forensic evidence from the Department of Justice investigation leaves us to deal with the hard truth that Mr. Brown was not just a victim. The evidence concludes that Mr. Brown was an aggressor and attributed to his own death. We might all agree that it may not have been necessary for Officer Wilson to kill him, but Mr. Brown's actions allowed Officer Wilson the freedom to decide how to apprehend him without consequence. Until I did the research I thought Michael Brown was another clear cut case of police brutality at its best. I'm pretty sure that many of you are also just now finding out that the opposite is true.

During this heightened period of confrontation and death between police and black people in 2016, society was terrified and traumatized, to say the least. With mostly, black men being murdered, black mothers, wives and sisters were in fear of their son's being killed, their husband's being killed, and their brother's being killed. The sentiment that emanated from television shows that covered the unbelievable rash of murders echoed "It is Hunting Season on the Black Man and black people in general."

Deep levels of hate for police begin to dominate social media posts, community discussions and barbershop conversations. Something had to be done to stop the madness and murder. Someone had to do something! Someone did! His name was Micah Johnson.

ONLY A MATTER OF TIME

It was a dark and dangerous day for every man and woman wearing a blue uniform in Dallas on July 7, 2016. This was the day that Micah Johnson, an Army reservist who had once served in Afghanistan, decided how he would balance a continuous wave of murder that police had executed against black people—black people who committed no crime at all, or who were at most, guilty of committing misdemeanors. His goal was to send a very disturbing wake up call to citizens, politicians, lawmakers, and police officers across the country.

The Army reservist who had served time in Afghanistan, outfitted himself with an arsenal of weapons including an SKS sniper rifle and took cover on the upper floor of a parking garage during a peaceful Black Lives Matter protest in honor of Alton Sterling and Philando Castile. Mr. Johnson had one goal in mind—to kill as many white police officers as possible.

The peaceful Black Lives Matter protest was cut short around 9pm when Mr. Johnson ambushed police from his sniper position. After the first few gunshots were fired, protesters ran to take cover. Some kept recording the chaos with their cell phones as it unfolded.

A gun battle between Mr. Johnson and the police spanned several blocks. The entire area went into lock down as the gun battle ensued. Then the live news reports started rolling in:

"We begin with Breaking News, multiple officers shot during a protest in downtown Dallas tonight...It is not clear exactly how many officers were shot."

CNN Affiliate KTVT Video 9:31 PM

"Breaking News: KTVT Report of two officers shot at Dallas protest"

CNN Video 11:23 PM

"Breaking News: Dallas Police: 11 officers shot, 4 killed"

Woman's voice:*"Oh my God, there are people lying on the ground. I hope they're just hiding."*

Multiple rounds of gunfire can be heard in the distance—

Man's voice:*"Somebody's armed, somebody is really armed to the teeth, this can't be one person."* [28]

The gun battle continued into the night. Mr. Johnson barricaded himself in the parking garage with plenty of ammunition and was still firing at officers. By the time he had taken some of his last shots, he had killed five officers and wounded seven others along with two civilians.

At one point the shooting stopped and the police were negotiating with Mr. Johnson to surrender. During negotiations Mr. Johnson claimed to have explosives planted in the area and that he planned to kill as many cops as possible.

> *"He said he was upset about the recent police shootings and that he was upset at white people. He stated he wanted to kill white people, especially white officers."*

> *"Negotiators spent hours trying to get him to surrender, Dallas Police Chief David Brown said, but it was a waste of time as he "told our negotiators that the end is coming and he's going to hurt and kill more of us...and that there are bombs all over the place in this garage and downtown."*

After making this statement police lost all hope of a peaceful surrender and negotiations broke down. Mr. Johnson had a final volley of gunfire with police before police deployed a remote controlled robot outfit with an explosive to kill him.

Citizens were left confused, anguished, and afraid as the night ended. The next day's New York Times Headline read:

"Five Dallas Officers Were Killed as Payback,

Police Chief Says"[29]

Micah's message, while horribly misdirected was heard loud and clear. Many black people felt the same anger he felt, but what he did was wrong. Just imagine if a black person who has not completely forgiven the U.S. for the slavery of black people decided that he would hang two random white men from a tree to retaliate for Thomas Shipp and Abram Smith (page 26). He would be absolutely wrong.

Mr. Johnson misdirected his hate to all police officers for the killings of Eric Garner, Tamir Rice, Freddie Gray, Sandra Bland, Alton Sterling, and other innocent black victims who had been murdered over the past few years. This was a fatal error, which in Mr. Johnson's mind, was rationalization for killing police officers who had nothing to do with the death of these innocent black victims. Mr. Johnson killed innocent officers who died in honor while protecting and serving their community. What Mr. Johnson failed to see was that there were many others who were to blame for these senseless killings that have continued. For example; the Mayor, the Police commissioner, politicians and political analysts who have not intervened to solve the root cause of the problem.

One thing that Mr. Johnson had correct was that all police enforcing the blue code of silence must be held accountable, but what he had wrong was that only those who pulled the triggers and killed innocent victims were responsible. Five Dallas police officers who were 950 miles away from the area where these victims were killed were not the blame and did not deserved to be killed.

In this instance Mr. Johnson's thinking was exactly the same thinking that occurs when racist police kill unarmed black citizens—*All black people are criminals and prepared to kill me, so if they make one false move they're dead.* This assertion is also undeniably wrong.

In the end, Mr. Johnson's reprisal did not change a thing and caused the senseless deaths of five police officers. Police abuse and violence towards black citizens continued after he ambushed police in Dallas that day. In fact, as this book was being written several more controversial killings of black civilians have occurred. Some of the higher profile cases include:

Eric Harris, 44, Oklahoma, 2 Apr 2016
Reason Killed: Deputy Meant to Fire Taser

Walter Scott, 50 South Carolina, 4 Apr 2015
Reason Killed: Fleeing from Officer

Tyre King, 13, Ohio, 14 Sep 2016
Reason Killed: Having a Toy Gun

Terence Crutcher, 40, Oklahoma, 16 Sep 2016
Reason Killed: Suspected of Having a Gun. Unsubstantiated

Keith Lamont Scott, 43, North Carolina, 20 Sep 2016.   Reason Killed:
Suspected of Having a Gun. Unsubstantiated

Police brutality in the United States has gotten so bad that other countries with a high population of People of African Descent have issued travel advisories associated with dealing with the police for individuals who plan to visit the U.S.

Following the shooting of Sterling, Castile, and Dallas police officers, the Bahamian government issued a travel advisory telling citizens to use caution when traveling to the U.S. due to racial tensions. They specifically advised that young men use "extreme caution" when interacting with police and to be non-confrontational and cooperative. Similar advisories were issued by the governments of United Arab Emirates and Bahrain days later.

If that wasn't bad enough, the UN issued a public statement on race relations and humanity with the U.S.

The Office of the United Nations High Commissioner for Human Rights (OHCHR) issued a statement strongly condemning Sterling and Castile's killings. Human rights expert Ricardo A. Sunga III, the current Chair of the United Nations Working Group of Experts on People of African Descent, stated that the killings demonstrate "a high level of structural and institutional racism" in the U.S., adding that "the United States is far from recognizing the same rights for all its citizens. Existing measures to address racist crimes motivated by prejudice are insufficient and have failed to stop the killings".[30 - 34]

REMEMBER ME

Akai Gurley 28

Brooklyn NY

Killed: Nov. 20, 2014

Crime: Unarmed. Shot in a dark stairwell of an East New York housing project building

Aftermath: District Attorney Ken Thompson announced that he is investigating.

AKAI IS WHY BLACK LIVES NEED TO MATTER

Photo Courtesy of Yahoo!

3

THE PARETO PRINCIPLE

"It's not like you are really listening to their words because you will key on what is the truth and what isn't. The first thing out of a ni**er's mouth for the first five or six sentences is a fuckin' lie."

-Mark Fuhrman
LAPD

On the morning of Sept 11, 2001 a tragic day was about to unfold. Murder, death, and tragedy were waiting. An act of war was about to be declared on American soil as two fully fueled 757 Jetliners and two fully fueled 767 Jetliners were hijacked and directed head on into their intended targets. Two of the Jetliners were flown into the North and South towers of the World Trade Center complex in New York City. Another Jetliner was flown into the Pentagon—the headquarters of the United States Department of Defense in Virginia. The last Jetliner was directed toward the White House in Washington, D.C., but crashed into a field in Pennsylvania after its passengers tried to overcome the hijackers.

Approximately 3000 people were killed and more than 6000 others injured. It was the deadliest incident for firefighters and law enforcement officers in the history of the United States. An estimated 343 firefighters and 72 law enforcement officers perished in the rescue effort.[35]

These first responders made the ultimate sacrifice while trying to save lives, and we can never repay them. The bravery and commitment they showed can only be compared with the sacrifice our military veterans have already made and the sacrifice that our enlisted military is currently making.

Sometimes our short-term memory causes us to forget about those who sacrificed their lives for us--people they don't even know. These heroes save people regardless of race, gender, or religious affiliation.

Several hundred firefighters and police officers heroically helped citizens get out of the burning World Trade centers and get to safety before they themselves perished beneath the falling concrete ruble. The firefighters and police officers that helped to save lives, upheld the oath they took. It did not matter to them whether the people they were rescuing were Black, White, Latino, Jewish, Muslim, or Catholic people. To these first responders we pay homage and are forever in their debt.

Of the hundreds of police officers who bravely served during this tragedy, seventy-two perished. These officers represent the type of civil servants we need policing our communities. They understood that their allegiance was to the people and that their oath was to, Protect and Serve The citizens, not themselves.

These men and women represent the Good officers who exist in each police unit. They mirror the true values of what America stands for. They wear the uniform proudly and represent the land of the free and the home of the brave.

These are not the *Bad* officers who turn a simple traffic stop into a victim's funeral.

These are not the *Bad* officers who choose a gun over a Taser to deal with children and the elderly.

These are not the *Bad* officers who use an illegal choke hold to subdue a suspect.

These are not the *Bad* officers who take the job personally and let their emotions, racial bias, and abuse of power cause a citizen's death.

These are the *Good* officers who first try to preserve life and only take it when absolutely necessary.

These are the *Good* officers who rushed to the scene of Columbine, Virginia Tech and Sandy Hook to rescue our precious children from harm.

These are the *Good* officers who put their lives in jeopardy to get the bad guys off the street.

These are the *Good* officers who have integrity and are accountable for their own actions.

These *Good* officers are a benefit to communities; they want to make positive change and care about the citizens they have sworn to protect.

There are approximately 343 million citizens living in the United States. If you were told that 65 million are criminals and they are making the other 278 Million productive members of society look like criminals, would that be hard to believe? Sixty-five Million is 20% of total population. This is likely the same ratio of Good and Bad that exists in every police precinct in America and is known as the Pareto Principle. In regards to police brutality, the appropriate statement is that 20% of the officers within a police department can cause a majority of the damage to the public image of a department. This damage becomes catastrophic when combined with the blue code of silence because citizens only see Good cops doing nothing to right the wrong while Bad cops get away with crime. This is exactly why most folks believe that there are no Good cops, but this is not true.

The country is currently at a critical inflection point as high ranking officers and concerned citizens are realizing that changes need to occur. This realization became abundantly clear when Chief Davis of the Dallas police department appeared on almost every major network the night Micah Johnson went on a police officer killing spree. With a sullen look on his face, Chief Davis looked directly into the camera and stated the following:

> *"We're hurting. Our profession is hurting. Dallas officers are hurting. We are heartbroken. There are no words to describe the atrocity that occurred to our city. All I know is that this must stop, this divisiveness between our police and our citizens."* [29]

At that moment he was letting us know that he realized just how much damage the racist and power hungry officers in each unit had caused.

Behind the scenes, Good officers are working to help repair the damage caused by the Bad officers. But their effort is not highly publicized by the media, as acts of goodness rarely make the news. Despite this fact, several officers are breaking ranks and are no longer honoring the blue code of silence. As you could imagine, their bravery has been met with anger from the Bad cops and is making other cops question everything they have been taught about police conduct.

The Pareto principle breakdown for police officers as previously stated is:

80% Good officers

20% Bad officers

The officers within the 80% Good officer category can be broken down into two sub-groups.

10% Blue Angels

70% Good Officers

Officers in the 70% category sub-group are officers who are generally Good officers who have not spoken out and crossed the thin blue line. The 10% sub-group are officers who make up the Blue Angel category. They are men and women of unimpeachable character, who deeply honor their oath. They have a conscience, they believe in the "Protect and Serve" creed, and they will not tolerate or support the code of silence. Officers Eddie Johnson, Nakia Jones, Joseph Crystal and Tommy Norman are a few officers who are in the Blue Angel category. They are the officers who bring honor, integrity, and respect to the badge and uniform.

Despite the backlash they have received and the disruption they are causing, Officers Eddie Johnson, Nakia Jones, Joseph Crystal and Tommy Norman have taken the lead to redefine the culture of law enforcement. They are modeling ethical behavior and holding officers accountable to the law enforcement code of conduct. These officers have made a commitment of bringing respect and honor back to the badge and to the blue uniform.

**Superintendent
Eddie Johnson**

**Chicago
Police
Department**

CPD Superintendent Eddie Johnson is taking a zero tolerance stance towards police misconduct with his recommendation that seven police officers be fired for filing false reports in the 2014 shooting of Laquan McDonald.

Mr. McDonald, a 17-year old African American youth was shot and killed as he was being pursued for breaking into trucks and stealing radios in a parking lot. The killing of Mr. McDonald, which was shown on CNN showed a wall of officers who had their guns drawn and ready to fire, lined up on the side of a road with Mr. Mcdonald walking in the middle of the road. Mr. McDonald appears to be walking away from the blockade of officers and police vehicles when one officer, Officer Jason Van Dyke, fired the fatal shots that killed Mr. McDonald. Before he fired, Officer Van Dyke stepped toward Mr. McDonald and fired his weapon. Once Mr. McDonald was hit, he spun around and fell to the ground twitching as his nervous system took over his muscles. While he was writhing on the ground, Officer Van Dyke discharged his weapon several more times into Mr. McDonald. Court documents state that Mr. McDonald had a knife with a three-inch blade on his person. Several officers who were at the scene reference the knife in their written testimony.

The reports that were filed by the officers were reviewed by the city's inspector general and an outside counsel. Reports, videos, and other evidence were reviewed and both investigators found that the officers involved violated Rule 14 of the Chicago Police Department's Rules and

Regulations. Rule 14 prohibits officers from making falsified written or oral reports that are used as evidence against citizens.

Here are a few examples of the falsified officer accounts that were refuted by video evidence.

The initial police portrayals of the incident, consisting of about 400 pages of typed and handwritten reports that prompted police supervisors to rule the case a justifiable homicide and within the bounds of the department's use of force guidelines. The reports stated that McDonald was acting "crazed" and lunged at officers after refusing to drop his knife.

Another police report described that McDonald "raised the knife across his chest" and pointed it at Van Dyke. Van Dyke told investigators that he feared McDonald would rush him with the knife or throw it at him.

One report also noted that McDonald's knife "was in the open position", but when announcing charges against Van Dyke, Cook County State's Attorney Anita Alvarez said the knife was found at the scene folded.[36]

These seven Chicago police officers are not the first officers to violate Rule 14. A separate investigation discovered twelve individual cases where Chicago police officers gave false testimony in court. The investigation also found that officers rarely, if ever, were held accountable for their actions.

Attorney and former Chicago Police officer (23 years on the job) and former independent police review board member (seven years on the job) Lorenzo Davis, was interviewed by Roland Martin. He stated that he was not surprised that Superintendent Eddie Johnson put forth a recommendation to fire the officers involved with Mr. McDonald's shooting and the subsequent cover-up. Mr. Davis told Roland Martin the situation in Chicago needed to be addressed.

"It finally got to that level where it had to be done. We're trying to change the police culture – a culture that has existed since before I was born – that culture of the code of silence. How else

can you change that without taking serious drastic measures?"[36]

Attorney Davis' career in law enforcement ended when he began to push for transparency in the cases he investigated as an independent police review board member. He was fired from the Independent Police Review Authority for insisting there be some accountability in the instances of unjustified police shootings and subsequently retired at the rank of commander, from the Chicago Police Department. [37]

Attorney Davis did his part to affect change, but he was met with roadblocks at every turn and was eventually fired. Despite his best efforts, the issues and circumstances that perpetuated unethical law enforcement communities remained. Racism, the code of silence, and abuse of power still permeated the primary culture within police departments.

Attorney Davis' push for better law enforcement practices within the Chicago Police department started a movement towards transparency within the department. There is still much work to be done, but Superintendent Eddie Johnson has stepped up and has taken over the reins leading the charge towards a more transparent, ethical police force. . His zero tolerance stance towards police misconduct is only the beginning of what he plans to do in order to finish what Attorney Davis started.

Officer Johnson, You have achieved Blue Angel status. On behalf of every citizen living in these United States of America, thank you for bringing a new level of accountability into law enforcement. And thank you for leading the way to better outcomes and safer communities for citizens and the honest, brave officers who proudly protect and serve their community, their state, and their country.

Officer Nakia Jones

Cleveland Police Department

Nakia Jones, a 20 year veteran of the Cleveland Police force, was deeply disturbed when her son came home and showed her the graphical social media video of two officers taking the life of Alton Sterling. She became increasingly angry as she repeatedly viewed the killing of Mr. Sterling, concluding that it was a completely unjustified murder perpetrated by racist police officers. The pain she felt was exacerbated by the fact that the officers who committed this public murder were from the same "family" that she was from. They wore the same uniform she wore and they took the same oath that she had taken. To express the deep pain and disappointment she was feeling, she uncharacteristically posted a seven minute video to verbally reprimand her fellow officers.

Initially, she spoke about why the video of Mr. Sterling being killed hurt her so deeply.

> *"I am so hurt right now. I try not to get into these conversations but I'm feeling so torn inside. I became a police officer in 1996 to help others to serve and protect my community, I started in the community I lived in which was East Cleveland. I wanted to give back."*

> *"It bothers me when I hear people say, 'Y'all police officers this, y'all police officers that.' They put us in this negative category when I'm saying to myself, 'I'm not that type of police officer,'"* she said.

"I know officers that are like me that would give their life for other people. So I'm looking at it, and it tore me up because I got to see what you all see. If I wasn't a police officer and I wasn't on the inside, I would be saying, 'Look at this racist stuff. Look at this.' And it hurt me." [38]

Then she angrily admonished the officers who killed Mr. Sterling.

"How dare you stand next to me in the same uniform and murder somebody! How dare you...! If you are white and you're working in a black community and you are racist, you need to be ashamed of yourself," she said. *"You stood up there and took an oath. If this is not where you want to work, then you need to take your behind somewhere else."*[38]

And finally in a solemn plea, she spoke to her community.

"Put these guns down because we're killing each other," she said. *"And the reason why all this racist stuff keeps going on is because we're divided. We're killing each other, not standing together."*[38]

She ended her very emotional address in tears. Her final words were:

"These are my thoughts, God bless." [38]

The bravery that Ms. Jones showed as she openly broke the unspoken rule of never going against her brothers and sisters in blue was confirmation that she is a model officer who really gives a damn! Officer Jones is a trailblazer. She undoubtedly will face backlash from her public reprimand of fellow officers. However, according to the mayor of Cleveland, Ms. Jones did not violate any policies by posting her video to facebook. She was not suspended or disciplined at the time, but she did receive threats from the Ku Klux Klan.

How the KKK became involved with a police matter remains a mystery. However, the Invisible Empire theory that was presented in the Cloaked Within chapter which establishes a link between police and a Klan-like subgroup of officers is one possibility.

Officer Jones, You have achieved Blue Angel status. On behalf of every citizen living in these United States of America, thank you for being the voice of the people. Thank you for being brave and going against the grain, and thank you for your service. Officers like you make America proud and allow the U.S. flag to blow in the wind with pride, integrity, honor, and loyalty.

Officer Joseph Crystal

Baltimore Police Department

Photo Courtesy of Yahoo!

Joseph Crystal, a former officer of the Baltimore police department put his integrity and love for being an officer over dishonoring his badge and following the culture of the code of silence. His refusal to support police brutality, and corruption left him isolated and ostracized within his unit. He was labeled a snitch, lost the respect and trust of almost every officer in his unit and was shunned at every opportunity.

Officer Crystal entered the police academy in 2008 and graduated with high achievement test scores. In 2009 he received a leadership award from the Mayor of Baltimore, given to trainees who showed the most leadership. He used his leadership skills to change the lives of the people who lived in some of Baltimore's poorest communities. While making a positive impact on Baltimore's residents, he felt that his service as a police officer was the most rewarding job ever.

Officer Crystal's intelligence and dedication allowed him to make Detective within the Violent Crimes Impact Section where he was tasked with getting guns and drugs off the street. He was working his dream job and everything was going well for him until the end of his shift on Oct. 27, 2011 when he was asked to make one more drug bust.

The drug bust was going to go down in a seedy area of Baltimore where it was common for drug deals to occur. Officer Crystal and two other officers approached the area and spotted a known drug dealer named Antoine Green. As soon as Mr. Green noticed the officers, he tossed a small bag of what appeared to be drugs on the ground. Then he took off running through a corridor of vacant houses.

The two policemen with Officer Crystal gave chase while Officer Crystal took charge of the squad car. To evade capture, Mr. Green kicked in the door of one of the houses in the corridor in order to find a place to hide. This decision turned Mr. Green's fate from bad to worse. Mr.Green had chosen a house that belonged to the girlfriend of an off-duty officer.

Shortly after entering and hiding inside the house, Mr. Green was apprehended by the two officers that were chasing him. Officer Crystal arrived at the house seconds later with the squad car and took position at the front door of the home. The other officers handcuffed Mr. Green and radioed for a police van to escort him to jail. One of the apprehending policemen subsequently called the boyfriend of the homeowner - an officer who was off duty at the time. He showed up shortly after the escort van left to take Mr. Green to jail.

Still on the scene, Officer Crystal and the apprehending officers explained to the off duty policeman how his girlfriend's home was damaged. Once the off duty policeman understood what had happened, he told one of the apprehending officers to radio the escort van driver to have the driver bring Mr. Green back to the home. When the escort van returned, Mr. Green was snatched out of the van and taken back into the home. As he was being forced into the home he started shouting, "They gonna fuck me up!"

The other officers had not told Officer Crystal Mr. Green was brought back to the house. All he knew was that he was supposed to stand guard at the front door again. The off-duty policeman and one of the apprehending officers dragged the handcuffed Mr. Green back into the house. Once they were just out of his view, officer Crystal could hear Mr. Green grunting and moaning for several minutes as the officers administered their own form of retribution for the damage Mr. Green did to the home of the off-duty officer's girlfriend. When they were finished beating Mr. Green, he was dragged back to the escort van. Officer Crystal noticed that Mr. Green's clothes were now ripped, torn and tattered and that he was unable to walk without limping. During the beating his ankle had been broken.

> *"They bring Mr. Green back and his shirt's ripped like he's fucking Hulk Hogan,"* Crystal said. *"He's limping on his ankle, which I later found out was broken. I honestly mean it when I say this: I never in a million years thought something like this would happen."* [39]

The following day, Officer Crystal went to his sergeant to report what he witnessed. In any other circumstance this would be the noble, ethical thing to do. Not in this case. Officer Crystal was ratting on his brothers in blue. Instead of receiving recognition he was beleaguered and harassed.

The sergeant told Officer Crystal to forget about what he had seen and to make sure internal affairs did not find out. Hearing those words from the sergeant left Officer Crystal confused and unsure what his duty to protect and serve actually meant. Officer Crystal felt worse when he read an incident report written by one of the apprehending officers.

It read:

> *"Once inside the wagon, Mr. Green calmed down and expressed a desire to apologize to the home owner for breaking into her home,"* the report said. *After he was taken back into the house, Mr. Green "attempted to charge and head-butt the home owners boyfriend who was an off-duty officer."* [39]

Besides this report sounding irrational, it is most likely a lie because the homeowner was not home during the break-in. It is highly unlikely that she showed up at home during the few minutes the police van left to take Mr. Green to jail.

Officer Crystal's loyalty and oath to protect and serve left him feeling guilty that he was a witness to police abuse and was unable to do anything about it. This is when he decided to get advice from someone outside of his unit. He set up an informal breakfast meeting with an Assistant State's Attorney to find out what he should do. Her advice was not that encouraging either. As he started to tell her what he had witnessed...

> *"She looks at me and says Joe if you continue to talk, I'm going to have to tell somebody so either tell me everything, or shut up and eat your goddamn pancakes!* [39]

It was apparent that the Assistant State Attorney was not really interested in the truth and did not want to get involved with a clear case of police abuse. But, Officer Crystal was unwilling to compromise his integrity and told her everything at that very moment.

> *"My whole career went to shit after that."* [39]

A few days after Officer Crystal gave his report to the State Attorney, two things happened:

1. An investigation was immediately opened by the State Attorney's Police Integrity Unit

2. Officer Crystal was labeled a "rat," because he did not uphold the code of silence

Over the next two years Officer Crystal was constantly harassed by other officers in his department, and his superior officers shunned him. His life in the unit was a living hell.

He documented the retaliation as it occurred and ended up with about 50 pages of notes. Here is some of what he endured:

> *"Do you want some cheese?" one sergeant asked Officer Crystal while offering him a hand-drawn picture of a block of cheese."*

In another incident, an officer pulled up to Crystal and yelled out of his window: "Hey, are you guys having a cheese party? I know rats like cheese!"

While out on assignments Officer Crystal said he would sometimes call for backup while pursuing suspects and his request for backup would be ignored.

In another instance Officer Crystal appealed to the president of the Baltimore Fraternal Order of Police to let him know that he was in fear of his safety and to request that the president review the log of harassment that he had been keeping. The president declined to review his notes and told Officer Crystal that the cops in his unit were mad at him because:

"It's blood in, blood out."

"Once you're in the unit, you die in the unit"

"What happens in the family stays in the family."

Officer Crystal responded to this by saying "They're mad at me because I went against the code?!. Then he replied "Are we fucking cops, or are we in a gang?! Which one is it?! You can't have it both ways!"

The Fraternal Order president responded to Officer Crystal by telling him that maybe he should look into joining a different police department.

On Thanksgiving Day, a week after speaking to The Fraternal Order president, Officer Crystal was at his home with his wife. He went outside to his car to get something and found a dead rat tucked under the windshield wiper.[39]

A year after Officer Crystal reported the incident, the two officers who beat the suspect were formally charged. This is when the harassment escalated.

A Lieutenant in the unit threatened Officer Crystal. "You are going to get charged with perjury when you testify. Your story better not change even a little bit."

The sergeant who Officer Crystal initially reported the incident to, threatened Officer Crystal by saying "You better pray to God you are not the star witness, because your career is already fucked! If you're the star witness, you may as well just resign."
[39]

In spite of the intimidation and harassment that Officer Crystal endured, the arresting officers were ultimately brought to justice. One of them was convicted of assault and obstruction of justice and sentenced to 45 days in jail. The other officer was convicted of misconduct and put on probation. Six months later, both officers left the force: One resigned, the other retired with a full pension. All charges against the suspect, Mr. Green, were dropped.

Officer Crystal resigned from the Baltimore Police force in 2014 after realizing that the retaliation, intimidation and harassment was not going to stop. He now works as a deputy sheriff in Walton County, Florida.

Officer Crystal, You have achieved Blue Angel status. On behalf of every citizen living in these United States of America, we thank you for your service and remain humbly in your debt. You are the definition of protect and serve.

Officer Tommy Norman

Arkansas Police Department

Photo Courtesy of Yahoo!

Tommy Norman is a patrol officer in the Arkansas Police Department whose social media notoriety has gone viral. Officer Norman has more than one million Facebook and one million Instagram followers who view his positive and uplifting interactions with residents of North Little Rock. He has transformed the people in his community into characters that social media followers have gotten to know through videos that he posts. It is common to see Officer Norman giving gifts to children that were sent from followers of his page. He might also be seen pretending to be the boyfriend of an older woman in the community who gets jealous when he tells her that he has to visit another one of his lady friends in the community. It's all done in good fun and allows viewers to see a police officer as a human being. By demonstrating that being a police officer is a multi-dimensional occupation that goes beyond upholding "the rule of law" to protecting and serving citizens, Officer Norman Shows that police officers are human and that they should care about their communities and the residents who live in them.

Officer Norman's launch as a celebrity was ironically bolstered by a well-known rapper who comes from the city of Compton where gang bangin' and cop hatin' go hand and hand. Los Angeles native The Game, formerly of the rap group G-Unit helped to make officer Norman a household name. He did this by telling his son to see if he could find a police officer who was making a positive impact on his community. The Game's son chose Officer Norman as that officer. To support Officer Norman's positive community policing campaign , The Game and his son launched a GoFundMe page and raised $66,000 to support Officer Norman's efforts.

In an Instagram post The Game wrote:

> *"I would have never in my life thought I'd be raising money on behalf of a police officer. I'm teaching my children and those who are watching to be better than we as a nation have been."*
> [40]

The Game deserves applause for teaching his son lessons in humanity and respect, but mostly he deserves applause in being able to change his own views towards law enforcement. If he can do it—anyone can.

Here is what Officer Norman had to say in an interview on Oct 21, 2016—

> *"My name is Tommy Norman, I'm a police officer in North Little Rock Arkansas. I work in the same city I was born and raised in. The people I work with in the community as a police office are all ages and races, from young to old. I think the initial reason I became a police officer was to arrest people and reduce crime. But once I became a police officer and realized the impact you could have through community policing, my vision changed. I do believe that being a police officer can change lives locally and depending on the platform that you have you can also impact lives across the globe. So with the position you have as a police officer the opportunities are endless as far as making a difference in people locally.*

> *There was a young man who was a teenager and I arrested him at McCain Mall, he was shoplifting. This was probably 8 or 9 years ago but he contacted me last year and he's now driving a truck across the world. He's making good money, he's supporting his family, but the reason he reached out to me was to let me know that because he felt like he was treated with dignity and respect when he was arrested, that made him realize that he*

had another chance in life. Now he is doing well for himself and his family.

When I do hear stories and see reports of people that lose trust in police officers and police departments it really makes me want to go out and make a bigger difference in the community and really go further when it comes to above and beyond—just to work even harder—to build more trust and respect. You know we're human beings and we do wear the uniform and drive a police car but we have a heart, we care about people and I think also the community and the public they have somewhat of an obligation to meet us halfway when it comes to forming these relationships. If you see a police officer walk up to him and start talking to him and just get to know him and a police officer should get to know you as well. We're friendly people and I think with the uniform, the badge and the gun some people may be intimidated by that figure and presence, but if you really get to know that police officer beyond that, you'd be really surprised." [41]

Officer Norman, You have achieved Blue Angel status. We need more officers like you to help us recover from the damage that has been done between U.S. citizens and our law enforcement community. It is true that we may never sit down at the table and eat dinner with each other, but through your leadership, the love of your job, the relationships you have with the children and the people you work with every day, we will at least know that it is an option. Thank you for opening our eyes and exposing us to a different side of what it means to be a police officer.

REMEMBER ME

Laquan McDonald, 17

Chicago, IL

Killed; October 20, 2014

Crime: Shot while walking away from a police officer.

Aftermath: Officer Van Dyke charged with first degree murder but released on bail. City reached settlement with family.

LAQUAN IS WHY BLACK LIVES NEED TO MATTER

Photo Courtesy of Yahoo!

Superintendent Eddie Johnson, Officer Jones, Officer Crystal and Officer Norman represent the top echelon of police officers around the country. They represent the best of the best officers that exist in law enforcement in our nation. You've most likely never heard about them because acts of valiance and kindness are not "newsworthy". The 24-hour news cycle in America is filled with reports of corruption, misconduct, and murder by law enforcement. Networks have done their market research and know that viewers will tune in for the violence and tragedy that these types of stories bring.

For all of the good that Superintendent Eddie Johnson, Officer Jones, Officer Crystal and Officer Norman have done, they have received little to no news coverage. If we as a society would demand that the media show something other than violence, and murder, we may achieve two critical changes that will help repair the contentious relationship between law enforcement and the general public:

First, this would help the public, communities, and citizens see that law enforcement in America has many other faces than what network television feeds us. Society needs to see and experience all aspects of law enforcement--The Bad as well as the Good.

Secondly, it would help law enforcement officers see that there are individuals within their ranks that have been brave enough to take a stand against police brutality, racism, and corruption. This may be the only motivation officers need to help them realize that they too should stand up for the truth.

Officer Norman stated that *"we care about people and I think also the community and the public they have somewhat of an obligation to meet us halfway when it comes to forming these relationships."*[41] Meet us halfway is a plea to the public. He is asking citizens to speak out and stand up against crime and to help strengthen our communities across our country.

Many of us are angry that police departments stand by and let racism and police abuse happen. If you are one of these angry people, yet you would not be willing to assist an officer in pursuit of a criminal, you must re-evaluate your anger towards the police. Community members and police officers need to work together as a team against police corruption and abuse. And like Officer Norman said, "We need to meet each other halfway."

PARETO PRINCIPLE CONTINUED

Earlier in this chapter we analyzed how the Pareto Principle applies to police and police brutality, we discussed how 20% of the officers within a police department can cause a majority of the damage to the public image of a department, and we defined how This damage becomes catastrophic when combined with the blue code of silence because citizens only see Good cops doing nothing to right the wrong. This exact same analysis is true when it is applied to black people and black communities as well.

During our law enforcement analysis, we showed that it is not logical to think that all police are Bad. It is equally illogical to think that all black people are Bad.

Every person reading this book needs to know that there are a large number of responsible and engaged black community members that are outraged when they see other black people looting their own neighborhoods and burning down stores as a result of their misguided anger towards law enforcement. The responsible citizens in the black community, who care about the neighborhood in which they live, are aggrieved by this type of destruction more than anyone else. Every time it happens, the reputation of all black people is tarnished and the entire black community pays for it. As with the police officers, it is approximately 20% of the black population who are responsible for casting a negative light on the entire race.

To prove that this is not speculation and show a clear correlation between the Pareto Principle and the black community, let's analyze a well-known New York City tenement known as the Queensbridge Houses; more commonly known as the Queensbridge projects.

The Queensbridge projects is the largest public housing development in North America. It contains a staggering 3000+ housing units and accommodates about 6000 residents of which 96% are minorities. Queensbridge projects were specifically built to house low to moderate income residents throughout the five boroughs of New York City.

Because of a once astounding level of crime, the project, which is more like a small city, has unfortunately been rubberstamped as the most corrupted project complex in New York City.

In 1986, Queensbridge had the most murders when compared to other NYC Projects. However, in recent years, life in Queensbridge has improved with a drastic overall drop in crime. According to Housing Authority statistics, there were no murders in 2004 but there were 25 assaults.[42]

An initiative by the NYPD contributed to the decreased crime rate.

In 2013 a New York Daily News article reported on an eight month police sting that was executed to apprehend criminals and increase safety within the Queensbridge projects. The NYPD arrested 40 suspects, ages 18 to 57, who had sold heroin, cocaine, oxycodone, methamphetamine and pot to undercover cops. This same article contained an interview from Carole Wilkins, the chair of the Queensbridge Project residence association, where she praised the efforts of the NYPD.

"I'm glad that the police are doing their jobs and keeping the community free from drugs," said Carol Wilkins, president of the Queensbridge Resident Association, which represents about 4,500 tenants. "I certainly hope this makes things better."[43]

If we make the following assumptions, we will see that the Pareto Principle applies:

- None of the Queensbridge Residents' Association members are drug dealers.
- Everyone that is not a member of the residence association is most likely a drug dealer

Approximately 6000 residents live in the Queensbridge projects. Of these residents, 4500 belong to the Queensbridge Resident Association. This means there are possibly 1,500 drug dealers operating in the Queensbridge Projects. The ratio of possible drug dealers to the total number of Queensbridge project residents is approximately 25%. This also means that approximately 75% of the residents in the Queensbridge Projects are not drug dealers. So the next time you look at a police officer, a black person, a white person, or any person for that matter; don't judge them by how they look—in fact, don't judge them at all. Just remember this chapter and reflect on the moment you realized that there are a small group of Bad people who exist in all cultures, races, shapes, sizes, religions, and occupations. These are the people who are making others look bad.

REMEMBER ME

Jonathan Ferrell 24

Bradfield Farms, NC

September 14, 2013

Crime: Ferrell crashed his car and knocked on the door of a nearby home to ask for help. The woman inside called the police instead of helping him. The Police arrived and shot Ferrell twelve times. Ferrell was unarmed at the time he was shot.

Aftermath: Officer Randall Kerrick has been indicted on a charge of voluntary manslaughter. It took two grand juries to get there.

JONATHAN IS WHY BLACK LIVES NEED TO MATTER

Photo Courtesy of Yahoo!

4

DEAD-END DIALOGUES

"You're a piece of shit fucking liar and I hope you fucking rot in hell. So fuck you. I hope I never fucking talk to you again ... You're a coward and a liar and a fucking ni**er alright, so fuck you!"

-Charlie Sheen
Actor

In the process of writing this book I have heard, have seen, and have participated in many discussions about police brutality and racism. Many of the discussions led nowhere, hence the chapter title; but there is one positive thing happening. We are talking with each other. For now that will have to do. Our next step in race relations is that we have to start listening to each other.

The dialogues that you will read are associated with racism and police brutality, and are not the exact conversations as they were heard, However, they are a close likeness. They will give you a window into the discourse in our society regarding race relations and police brutality. The discussions are documented under the names of two fictitious characters. An African American character named A. Black and a White American character named A. White.

SANDRA BLAND

A. Black	*There have been way too many police killing black people recently.*
A. White	*If those people who were killed followed police instructions, they would not have been killed.*
A. Black	*Several of them did follow instructions and they still ended up dead—like what happened to Sandra Bland.*
A. White	*She committed suicide. You can't hold the police responsible for her death.*
A. Black	*The coroner's report lists suicide as the cause of death, but logically it does not make sense. And anyway, her death was a result of a ridiculous traffic stop.*
A. White	*I saw the video. She resisted arrest.*

A. Black	*If you saw the video, please refresh my memory of why she was getting arrested. I'm still confused about that.*
A. White	*She had a broken turn signal and the officer was well within his rights to pull her over.*
A. Black	Let's say I agree with your point. Doesn't she get a ticket for that? She should have received a citation and she should have been on her way. Instead she was found three days later hanging dead in a jail cell. Let's forget that she was black for a moment, doesn't it concern you that this type of thing could happen at all?
A. White	*When the officer told her to get out of the car, she should have followed his instructions.*
A. Black	I think you missed the point. She was pulled over for a broken turn signal. What reason is there to ask her to get out of her car? She should have received a ticket and she should have been on her way.
A. White	*She was high anyway. They found a large quantity of marijuana in her system during the autopsy. Speculation is that she swallowed it before she was arrested.*

| A. Black | *I read those same notes from the autopsy report and what you didn't state is that she was in jail for three days. Even the coroner thought something was strange about this. No one could have that much* |

	THC in their system after being in jail three days. This fact alone supports a cover-up. And even if she was high, did she deserve to be murdered?
A. White	*There you go again. Where is the proof she was murdered?*
A. Black	*I don't have definitive proof, but I have common-sense and if she wasn't murdered I would think that the jail where she was held would be offering up its own proof to exonerate its personnel.*
A. White	*So now you can just make claims without proof? That is not how the judicial system works. You don't have a video or tape with a jail guard murdering her. The coroner has classified her death as a suicide. She was combative with the officer who stopped her. She probably was the same way in jail.*

MIKE BROWN

A. White	*What the hell is wrong with your people in Ferguson? They are looting and destroying their own community?*
A. Black	*The police department is corrupt. They just killed an innocent 18 year-old boy that was surrendering. He had his hands in the air. They've had enough. People are pissed off. One month ago some racist, power hungry cops killed Eric Garner for nothing. Enough is enough!*
A. White	*So looting and ruining your own property will fix the problem? Real smart.*

A. Black	*I'm not saying I condone it, but I understand. It is misdirected dysfunctional anger. I get it. I can see why you will never understand. You live in your protected white privilege plastic bubble. Until you have lived in America as a black person you won't understand.*
A. White	*I don't need to be black in America to know that ruining your own community is stupid. And how do you know the cops in Ferguson are racist? Every time there is a white cop and black victim, black people are quick to blame racism.*
A. Black	*You say that, but I bet you wouldn't last a day dealing with the circumstances that I do. You want to know why racism is our first reaction? Have you heard of a little thing called slavery. I bet you think slavery also had nothing to do with racism.*
A. White	*That was over four hundred years ago. Slavery has nothing to do with today. You get the same rights and opportunities as me. Stop whining about the past and let's discuss why your people are tearing their own town apart.*

A. Black	*You must be a straight idiot if you really believe what you just said. Slavery has everything to do with today. It is the basis and foundation that shaped today. It's a shame that you are quick to discount a time in history that outlines the worst case of racism that occurred in America. Are you that quick to write off the Holocaust too? And are you kidding me! You think I have the same opportunities as you. Unbelievable! Why do you think Affirmative Action is in place today?*

A. White	It's to make sure companies fill a quota with a specific number of black employees.
A. Black	Not even close. Affirmative Action is in place to make sure that a diverse pool of candidates is considered for a particular job. Without it, black people might not even end up in the pool of consideration. I can't believe that it is this difficult for you to recognize that the playing field is not equal. Mike Brown is dead for this very reason. If he was a white man the officers first priority would have been to take him to jail alive. Do you remember Dylan Storm Roof? He was that white teen that shot and killed nine black people during a bible study meeting at a church in South Carolina. He killed nine people and had a gun yet he was taken into custody without incident. Mike Brown stole some cigarillos and was shot dead where he stood.
A. White	Are you living under a rock? Did you read the Department of Justice report on Mike Brown? He was not some innocent victim or the sweet teenager that his friends and people in the town made him out to be. He bullied a store attendant, stole cigarillos and assaulted a cop. What did you think would happen?

A. Black	How come every time a black person gets killed, the first thing your people do is dive into his background and do a resume check?
A. White	We do that because blacks are 13% of the U.S. population and they account for 50% of violent crimes.
A. Black	Do me a favor and find the statistics on white collar crime. You know, the kind of crime that is not tracked. The kind of crime that gets renters kicked

	out of their homes because the owner, who was not properly screened by a greedy bank, could not pay the mortgage and left the renters to get kicked out by the sheriff. Let's see what the percentage breakdown for white and black is regarding this type of crime
A. White	*I'm not even following you anymore. All I know is that if you read the Department of Justice report, you will see that DNA evidence proves that Mike Brown contributed to his own death. There was no hands in the air, I surrender moment, like your Black Lives Matter people said. The entire hands in the air thing was drummed up to purposely incite opposition against the police.*
A. Black	*So now all of this is the fault of the Black Lives Matter movement. I shouldn't be surprised that you said that though. It's just 1963 all over again. But instead of blaming Martin Luther King for the world's problems, white people are blaming the Black Lives Matter movement.*

OFFICER MISCONDUCT 1

A. White	*....Exactly! Statistics show that police officers kill more whites than blacks from year to year and based on the population of each ethnic group the number of killings is actually pretty small.*
A. Black	*If it is true that police kill more whites than blacks, how come I have not seen a White Lives Matter movement or any protest of these killings?*
A. White	*A movement for what. In a country with 326 Million people there are bound to be people who die as a*

	result of enforcing laws.
A. Black	*How many of the white people who were killed while dealing with police were killed while in the act of committing a crime and how many were killed for no reason at all?*
A. White	*Police don't kill people for nothing. If a person ends up dead, it is because they were doing something they should not have been doing.*
A. Black	*You live in a perfect world. That is not how things work in the real world. John Crawford III was killed because someone called the police and lied on him. They reported that he was walking through Walmart with a gun pointing it at people. After he was dead they discovered that he was actually carrying a pellet gun. What about that?*
A. White	*I don't have all the facts but if Police had to shoot him, I'm sure there was a reason.*

A. Black	*He was in Walmart. Maybe he was shopping and was going to buy the pellet gun.*
A. White	*The officer was doing his job. He most likely thought the man was going to harm someone so he took action.*
A. Black	*Very reminiscent of George Zimmerman and Trayvon Martin. Zimmerman thought Trayvon who was living in the same housing complex that he lived in, was a threat, so he took action. Zimmerman killed Trayvon Martin during a struggle in which he was overpowered and pulled a gun. This should clearly indicates that rational thought must be used before*

	someone's life is taken.
A. White	*You obviously have never been a police officer. Sometimes you only get a matter of seconds to put down a possible threat or innocent victims get hurt. And since you brought up George Zimmerman, he had his day in court and was acquitted.*
A. Black	*No I have not been a police officer. I also have not been a doctor, but I know that if a healthy person came to my office for a medical procedure and they ended up dead as a result of my actions that I would be evaluated as to whether I was fit to continue as a doctor. My point is that a reckless person is not someone who should be trusted with human life. The same should apply for police officers. And by the way, O.J. Simpson had his day in court too and was acquitted. Did you think he was innocent after his trial?*

A. White	*You talk tough, but I bet if you had to run towards bullets like police do you would change your tone and not be so critical of police. Really, did you just bring up O.J. Simpson? Everyone knows he was guilty.*
A. Black	*I don't dispute that the police have a tough job, but you must admit that people have died under very questionable circumstances and there is usually no evidence to prove otherwise. If the people being killed were police, I am sure that no expense would be spared in order to bring the perpetrator to justice.*
A. White	*I know, don't tell me, all police are bad right?*

REMEMBER ME

John Crawford III 22

Beavercreek OH

Killed: August 5, 2014

Crime: Crawford was fatally shot by police while carrying a pellet gun in a Walmart. A man named Ronald Ritchie told 911 that Crawford was pointing it at people in the Walmart, but a month later he admitted that Crawford was not pointing the gun at shoppers in the Walmart.

Aftermath: No indictment.

JOHN IS WHY BLACK LIVES NEED TO MATTER

A. Black	*I just saw a video of a black high school girl who was sitting at her desk get man handled. She was dumped out of her desk and thrown across the room by a white resource officer.*
A. White	*I saw that video too. What it didn't show was what happened before the video started.*
A. Black	*What action in your mind would justify throwing a high school girl across a classroom?*
A. White	*Oh she did something. I'm sure of that.*
A. Black	*She did do something. The teacher told her to stop texting in class and asked for her phone. She refused to give it up.*
A. White	*The teacher's know the rules of the class. If they call a resource officer it means that someone is breaking the rules and they need help enforcing them.*
A. Black	*She didn't rob a bank, have a gun or have drugs! She refused to give up her cell phone. Are you getting this?*
A. White	*What did the teacher and school administrators have to say about the incident?*

A. Black	*They thought the officer's actions were justified. Does that really matter?*
A. White	*Of course it does. He works for them. If they felt he did the right thing, then he did.*
A. Black	*How can you say that when you don't have the entire story?*
A. White	*I don't need it. She broke the rules.*
A. Black	*So in your book when people break the rules anything goes?*
A. White	*Why wouldn't that be the case?*
A. Black	*I've never heard anything so absurd. They could have just asked the girl to leave class or they could have called her parents or something.*
A. White	*The teacher, resource officer and administration are not there to babysit. They are all there to support the process of teaching the kids. They don't have time for all of that.*
A. Black	*Well I'm happy to let you know that the resource officer was fired.*
A. White	*That's garbage. He did the job he was getting paid to do.*

A. Black	*The article that I read stated that the use of violence and excessive force by teachers and staff members to make students comply is a fireable offense (if the parents press charges he could go to jail).*
A. White	*If the student's conduct was bad enough to call the resource officer then he was needed to do something beyond what the teacher could do. It doesn't make sense that he was fired. Just fire all the resource officers then and let the teachers deal with the madness.*
A. Black	*If that was your daughter you would be cursing the resource officer and lobbying to have him fired too.*
A. White	*My daughter would not be in class acting like this girl did. I've taught her to respect teachers and authority.*
A. Black	*Yeah right. You've raised a perfect little angel. The first time you tell her that she cannot go to a party or that she cannot have a boyfriend, you will find out just how perfect she is. And everyone can have a bad day, maybe that was her problem. What makes you think that her parents didn't teach her to be respectful?*

BLACK LIVES MATTER

A. White	*Explain why Black Lives Matter only came about when police killed a few black people? How come that group wasn't up in arms because of all the black on black crime that exists?*
A. Black	*Black on black crime and police killings of blacks at a disproportionate rate are not even related. The only common thread is that they are both crimes. In the cases where the police are involved, the citizen is not committing a crime or trying to hurt anyone. The citizen ends up dead and the officer ends up on paid leave. When it comes to black on black crime, someone may end up dead, but the other person is going on trial to defend his life.*
A. White	*You said that like Black Lives Don't Matter.*
A. Black	*I just know that black on black crime is no worse than white on white crime, green on green crime, blue on blue crime...etc. Statistically you are more likely to get killed by someone of the same race.*
A. White	*Even if that is true, a lot of your people are killed by shooting each other. In places like Chicago black people are killed on a constant basis by other black people. How about telling your Black Live Matter group to focus on that first. It is the larger of the two issues.*

A. Black	*Do you even know what the Black Lives Matter movement is about?*
A. White	*Yeah. They loot stores when a black person is killed, they walk on the highway and shut down traffic, and they escalate racism issues against an already unstable black and white social structure.*
A. Black	*ot even close. Time for a lesson; I want to make sure that you will never reiterate that stupidity that I just heard.* *lack Lives Matter is an international activist movement that was started in the African-American community in 2013. The main purpose of the group is to campaign against violence and systemic racism toward black people. Most recently, due to the high occurrence of police killing African-Americans, the group's main focus has been to protest police killings of black people that occurred due to police brutality.*
A. White	*Oh now I get it. This explains why they only pop up when the conflict is a white versus black issue.*
A. Black	*You make it sound like they are the racists. They aren't. Their goal is to put racism out of business.*
A. White	*Every issue that occurs between whites and blacks is not necessarily racially motivated, however, this group likes to make it seem that way.*

A. Black	*I can see how it could look that way to people that flat out deny any wrongdoing by police officers. The people who do this could not recognize or maybe they don't want to acknowledge racism when it*

	occurs.
A. White	*Maybe if you guys pull your pants up, obey the law and show police officers some respect, you might get treated better.*
A. Black	*I don't know where you came up with that garbage but let me tell you this—racists don't care how you dress, they don't care if you show respect, and it never crosses their mind to treat black people fairly. On top of that, I give respect when it is due, not because I feel threatened. And also, take a good look at how the young white suburbanites are wearing their pants today.*

SLAVERY

A. White	*How come every time I talk to a black person they ultimately relate all the disadvantages that they have in life back to slavery? Didn't the 13th Amendment fix all this? When will your people take personal responsibility?*
A. Black	*So if you chopped my foot off 20 years ago and today we race and I lose, you would consider it a cop-out if I said "With my other foot I would have won even though you chopped it off", is that right?*
A. White	*Life is not fair, everyone must deal with his or her circumstances. It's not ok to keep whining and making excuses.*
A. Black	*I guess "making excuses" is what you call anything that puts your people in a bad light. Why don't you just admit that in a time before you existed, your*

	people took advantage of and mistreated another group of people and that they were wrong for doing it?
A. White	*How can you even make the inference that I have ownership of what happened over 400 years ago? I wasn't there, I didn't do it. The past is the past. You don't see Jewish people still asking German people to admit that they did something wrong.*
A. Black	*First of all, I totally disagree with you that—the past is the past. In fact, lets apply that statement to the Jewish people who experienced the tragedy related to the genocide of "undesirable people." If you asked a Jewish person if their people have recovered from the Holocaust, the answer you would most likely receive is the following:* *"To some extent we have never recovered. I don't think anyone can say that our community has recovered. How can a community, a people, recover from something as traumatic, as horrific as the Holocaust? There is a phrase used in connection with the Holocaust that comes to mind—the abomination of desolation—the feeling of being unwanted and hated, and for no good reason.* *If there is a chance that you have empathy for the Jewish people, perhaps you can understand the plight of black people.*
A. White	*Are you really comparing slavery to the Holocaust? The Jews had it much worse. You are comparing apples and oranges.*
A. Black	*It is futile and disrespectful to both groups to measure whether Jewish people or black people suffered more. Both dealt with unimaginable atrocities and if you look at the magnitude of death, you will find that approximately 13 Million Jews died during the Holocaust and that 100 Million black people died during slavery. Why you are able to understand and feel the pain of 13 Million and not*

	100 Million, boggles my mind.

BLUE LIVES MATTER

A. Black	*You mean the feelings of anger only just now showed up because the police in Dallas were killed? What about all the black people that have recently gotten killed for pretty much no reason? This didn't make you mad?*
A. White	*All I'm saying is that those cops were there to keep law and order at a Black Lives Matter event. They had done nothing wrong and they were shot down like animals because of the uniform that they wore.*
A. Black	*This sounds like a familiar argument that I presented to you. Let's take Yvette Smith from Bastrop Texas for example: she was killed by police who were responding to a domestic disturbance call when she opened the front door of her home. Her crime was opening her front door. Maybe now you are starting to get it.*
A. White	*The murder of these five cops was deliberate.*
A. Black	*So what do you think it was that put Micah Johnson in the state of mind to randomly kill cops? Do you think he just woke up one morning in a psychotic rage and decided that his target would be police officers?*
A. White	*He was following that Black Lives Matter nonsense—they have a hate whitey agenda. He probably was just brainwashed and was planning to kill white people anyway. The police abuse and racism claims*

	fueled by the media just gave him an excuse to hide behind.
A. Black	*You stay in denial. You know that Micah Johnson was fed up with all the black people who were unjustifiably killed by police. He was fed up with black people being killed and police officers not being held accountable, he was fed up with the power structure standing by and letting the racism and police abuse continue. This was payback! Even the Houston police chief said it was.*
A. White	*And you guys wonder why we see you as a threat. Trust me when I say that Micah only made the itchy trigger fingers in the police department more sensitive. His actions did not fix the problem.*
A. Black	*Perhaps, but maybe he saved a few black lives. If police realize that their lives can be taken as well, maybe the racist cops and the police who exercise abuse of power will think twice before killing another black person without justification. Also, his action might motivate the police who stand idly by when an officer does something wrong, to speak up and break the code of silence. If you review the biblical pages of Exodus and Leviticus you will find a well-known idiom that states "An eye for an eye."*
A. White	*And finally we have it! Out of one side of your mouth you keep talking to me about how many black people have been killed by cops and that you don't like it, out of the other you quote "An eye for an eye." Which is it? Stop killing or kill everyone? You can't have it both ways.*
A. Black	*It's not my decision to make. It's not like I instructed Micah Johnson to do what he did, but I certainly understand. I felt like doing exactly what he did when day after day all I was hearing about was black people getting killed.*

A. White	*Then why didn't you?*
A. Black	*I have a family. I have people that depend on me so deciding to throw my life away is not an option.* *So let me ask you. You were watching all the killings that were happening before the officers were killed. Did you not think that there would be retaliation?*

REMEMBER ME

Terrence Crutcher, 40

Tulsa, OK

Killed; September 16, 2016

Crime: Shot by officer Shelby while unarmed next to his automobile for refusing to follow police commands.

Aftermath: On May 15, 2017 Officer Shelby found not guilty of first degree manslaughter.

TERRENCE IS WHY BLACK LIVES NEED TO MATTER

Photo Courtesy of Yahoo!

TRUMP

A. Black	*Today is November 9th, 2016 and I would like to ask you how in the hell did your people allow a demagogue like Donald Trump become president?*
A. White	*First of all, it is a little presumptuous of you to think that I voted for him, but let's say I did, I bet that even with no experience that he is going to do a better job than president Obama.*
A. Black	*I doubt that, but the bigger issue is that Donald Trump essentially ran a hate campaign and won the presidency. He openly showed racism against Mexicans and Muslims, he degraded and verbally assaulted women, he ran a high school smear campaign to assassinate the character of his opponents and attacked them on a personal level, he trumped up (no pun intended) conspiracies for followers to glom onto, and dragged the presidential candidacy through the gutter. This is your chosen candidate. Don't deny it. Defend your new president.*
A. White	*There is nothing to defend. Donald Trump won because people are tired of politicians that talk a good game and don't follow through with results. People are tired of Mexicans who keep coming into the U.S. illegally and abusing our amnesty policies just because they have had children on U.S. land, people are tired of Muslims coming into our country to wait as a sleeper cell so they can blow-up and kill Americans, people are tired of a broken Obama care medical system that isn't working. This is why Trump won and you damn right I voted for the man!*
A. Black	*So you embrace the racism and hate?*

A. White	*You can say that if you want, but before you do answer these questions:*
	Is there a problem with illegals at the U.S./Mexico border?
	Have Muslims killed innocent U.S. citizens
	These are the people causing the problem so it is not racism--it is the truth!
A. Black	*One question: Before 911 occurred do you know the nationality of the man who perpetrated the worst case of terrorism on U.S. soil? I will just let that simmer right there.*
A. White	*You can throw up smoke and mirrors and conspiracy theories all you want. That doesn't change the fact that the issues I presented are true.*
A. Black	*Let's say they are. Can we talk about the fact that never in the history of the presidency has a candidate been hated more by his own countrymen or laughed at and feared by those on foreign soil. That should mean something.*
A. White	*The people have spoken.*
A. Black	*The people did speak but their voices were not heard. Hillary Clinton won the popular vote, but unfortunately elections follow this ridiculously complicated electoral college process that hasn't been changed since the 1700's which very few people understand.*
A. White	*Funny how you didn't have a problem with the system when your candidate won, but now you do?*

KAEPERNICK

A. White	*I think people that don't honor the American flag are a disgrace to the United States and should be brought up on treason charges.*
A. Black	*So do I.*
A. White	*Finally, something we agree with. So you agree that Colin Kaepernick should be charged.*
A. Black	*No I don't agree with that. Kaepernick is exercising his first amendment right to peaceful protest. He is not disrespecting the flag. I've seen people burn and desecrate the flag. Those people are the individuals that are committing treason.*
A. White	*But he is disrespecting the country and our military by refusing to stand. This should not be allowed.*
A. Black	*That is not disrespecting the country and military. When you enlist in the military to serve your country, you take an oath to support and defend the constitution. No matter how unpopular or controversial an individual's actions may be, each individual has a constitutional right to peacefully protest in order to bring attention to an issue that he feels strongly about.*
A. White	*If you live in this country then you should support this country. Standing up for our national anthem shows you support our country. If you do not stand then you do not support this country.*
A. Black	*Not necessarily. Military personnel have come forward in support of Kaepernick's protest. They actually made statements that they proudly serve*

	this country to allow people to exercise their constitutional right to protest.
A. White	*I don't care what you say, he is being disrespectful to all the men and women who died to make this a great country when he does not respect the flag. This country has given him the opportunity to be a millionaire and live an affluent lifestyle. In his case it is even more apparent how great our country is because he belongs to an elite group of one percenters. He makes a ton of money, lives a good life and wants for nothing. He should respect the flag and the fact that being an American citizen is one reason why he is in this unique situation.*
A. Black	*Everything you said may be true, but it is beside the point. Kaepernick is using his privileged position to shed light on police brutality against black and brown people. He has decided that living a comfortable life must come second to the pain and anguish of others. He watched time and time again as black people were being treated less than human and being gunned down for little to no reason. He watched as mayors, police commissioners and legislatures did nothing to stop the obvious racism and police abuse against black people. This is why he takes a knee and not because he is a disrespectful individual.*
A. White	*He should just stick to playing football and let civil rights activists deal with the racism issues.*
A. Black	*Historically sports figures have been instrumental in bringing attention to issues that plague our nation. Do you remember a sports figure named Muhammad Ali? Do you remember how involved he was in bringing attention to the plight that black people were facing in the U.S? He used his platform to speak out against the war in vietnam and highlight that it was not right to ask a people who don't have equal rights in America to go abroad and*

	fight.
A. White	*He went to jail for that too. Maybe Kaepernick should go to jail just like he did.*

WHY AM I BEING DETAINED

A. Black	*The thing I don't understand is why police don't just let individuals know what they've done prior to being arrested.*
A. White	*Why does it even matter? When you are stopped by a police officer he can detain you. Police ask the questions they don't answer questions.*
A. Black	*I see. I think you just answered my question. It's all about abuse of power. Why is stopping someone who is walking on the street or in a mall any different from being pulled over for a speeding ticket? The reasons are the same. When an individual is pulled over or stopped while walking, the police officer is required to follow certain procedures during the detention process - which includes letting you know why are abe being stopped or detained. The police officer's failure or refusal to do this is an abuse of power.*
A. White	*Look, the rules are simple. The process is simple. When an individual is stopped by a police officer he should follow all commands given by the officer, not resist arrest, and not make any sudden moves. By doing this the officer can control any existing threat so that he can properly deal with the individual being apprehended. If these simple rules are*

	followed citizens can avoid being hurt or killed in the process. I personally don't see why doing this is so hard.
A. Black	*Do your rules apply to all ethnicities or is that just for the brown people?*
A. White	*These rules apply to everyone.*
A. Black	*I've seen several automobile stops where white people were stopped and they did not follow those rules and no one was hurt or killed. I think your rules only apply to certain groups of people and not others because I have also seen where black people have followed those rules and ultimately they were still hurt or killed.*
A. White	*I think you are mistaken. I guarantee you that in every case you are talking about the individual resisted arrest or made a move that made the officer feel threatened.*

THINGS DON'T ADD UP

A. Black	I'm sure you heard the latest lies coming from the police department about the Botham Jean murder?
A. White	I heard about it and I think that the door was either left ajar or was slightly open and when she went up to the door thinking that it was her apartment, she did what any alert police officer would have done.
A. Black	Whoa! Back it up some. First you are way too far into the issue. Let's examine the facts. 1.) She parked her car on the the wrong floor 2.) She went to the wrong apartment 3.) She did not notice the red rug 4.) The door just happened to be open 5.) She gave Mr. Jean commands and shot him because she thought her life was in danger. You want me to believe that all this happened because the officer worked a 16 hour shift that she no longer knew what floor she lived on and that she was delusional? Is that what you want me to believe?
A. White	Look, the rules are simple. The process is simple. When a police officer gives you a command you should follow them. It doesn't make a difference whether or not you are in your own apartment or someone else's apartment. You should follow all commands given by the officer, not resist arrest, and not make any sudden moves. By doing this the

	officer can control any
	existing threat or potential threat. If these simple rules are followed citizens can avoid being hurt or killed in the
	process. I personally don't see why doing this is so hard.
A. Black	*Her police Captain said she was getting off of work, so was she there as a Police Officer or as a citizen?*
A. White	*It doesn't make a difference. She is a police officer and her job is to protect and serve. She saw a potential crime in progress and did the right thing.*
A. Black	*This must be a new crime... Black while in your own apartment! Cut the crap, you know there is a cover-up in progress.*
	Ok so let's say I buy your garbage, explain how she did not notice the red rug at the front door?
A. White	*I think you are mistaken about the red rug, but that is not important. The important thing is that she went into the*
	apartment to prevent a possible crime. It's not like she knocked on the door and was let in by the person who lived there,
	like one of the tenants of the building said.
A. Black	*I'm no genius, but crimes are usually preceded by a 911 call. So what was the crime she was investigating? How come*
	this has not been offered as a theory to this murder?
A. White	*So now you are saying that she let herself into the apartment and shot the victim because she knew*

	him?
A. Black	*Uhhhhh.....Yeah! That is the current narrative. I see they have already started their smear campaign and are reporting findings of marijuana in his apartment. How come they have not searched her apartment. You know the one she was supposed to go to?!*
A. White	*There is no evidence to support a need to search her apartment. It's not like they knew each other and were having some type of lovers quarrel that turned violent as the media is now trying to portray from the fact that the victims dying words were, "My God, what have you done."*
A. Black	*You are doing the same thing the police department is doing...shining the light on the wrong issues instead of* *dealing with the facts...* *She went to the wrong floor in her building* *She went to the wrong apartment* *She missed noticing the red rug* *She was off-duty and acting like an officer* *She shot and killed an innocent person who was not in the commission of a crime* *For once let's focus on the facts!*
A. White	*So now you are saying that she set it up to have access to his apartment, knew when he would be home so she could go in and shoot him? Maybe you think she was in cahoots with his marijuana dealer?*

REMEMBER ME

Walter Lamar Scott, 50

North Charleston, SC

Killed; April 4, 2015

Crime: Shot from behind by police officer Michael Slager while fleeing a daytime traffic stop

Aftermath: Michael Slager sentenced to 20 years in prison based upon a plea agreement. Scott family received 6.5 million in an-out-of-court settlement.

WALTER IS WHY BLACK LIVES NEED TO MATTER

Photo Courtesy of Yahoo!

FALLACIES

In addition to the thought provoking value of this chapter, you may have noticed that two people engaged in the highly-charged, race related discussions had a difficult and frustrating time seeing the other's point of view. Within the dialogue you may have noticed one or both participants making a claim without considering all the evidence, and without questioning their own biases and assumptions.

These dead end dialogues are due to a phenomenon called "Blindspotting". Blindspotting occurs "when a situation or an image can be interpreted in different ways, but an individual only sees one of the interpretations. This individual has a "blindspot" to the other interpretations. When this happens a person maintains a singular view of a situation that can have other possible causes and this can manifest into disjointed rhetorical conversation like you've just read.

Because Blindspotting allows us to have limited insight and understanding of multiple sides of an argument, it leads to fallacies, or "a mistaken belief, especially one based on unsound argument". In 40. B.C, the great philosopher Aristotle did an analysis of rhetoric that explains this behavior in clear concise context. His analysis produced thirteen fallacies that map to the main causes of why individuals use rhetoric when debating.

In this section we will map each dead-end dialogue to one of Aristotle's fallacies and provide reasoning of why the conversation failed.

SANDRA BLAND DISCUSSION

Aristotle Fallacy: The Fallacy of Accident

Basic Definition: The general idea of Fallacy of Accident is that the individual who is speaking about an incident applies illogical reasoning to a unique situation

Analysis: In the Sandra Bland discussion A. Black starts a conversation about the number of black people that have been getting killed. His discussion includes Sandra Bland. Sometime later A. White attempts to justify Sandra Bland's death.

A. White's blindspot was the fact that Sandra Bland's death was not a natural consequence of being in jail and results with him applying illogical reasoning to this unique outcome.

MIKE BROWN DISCUSSION

Aristotle Fallacy: The Fallacy of-Missing the Point

Basic Definition: The general idea of Fallacy of Missing the Point is that an individual makes an argument to prove a point but instead proves a point to something unrelated to the conversation.

Analysis: In the Mike Brown discussion A. White starts a conversation about black people destroying property in the community in which they live. A. Black attempts to explain that the destruction of property is the result of Mike Brown being killed.

A. White's blindspot is the fact that he does not see that looting and rioting is an expression of moral outrage and that Mike Brown's death is a concern for the community.

A White's argument that rioting and looting will not fix the problem changes the focus from Mike Brown's death to the destruction of property within the black community. This is how he misses the point.

OFFICER MISCONDUCT #1 DISCUSSION

Aristotle Fallacy: The Fallacy of – In a Certain Respect and Simply

Basic Definition: The general idea of Fallacy of - In a Certain Respect and Simply occurs when an attribute that may be true in one instance is applied to a wider domain than originally intended.

Analysis: In the Officer Misconduct #1 discussion, *A. White makes the assumption that all people killed by police are doing something wrong. This is not true, sometimes police are at fault because of accident or an error in judgment that places an individual in a situation where being killed becomes the only outcome.*

A White's blindspot is that there are other reasons why an individual could be killed by a police officer. A. White's statement is only true for some cases, but not all.

OFFICER MISCONDUCT #2 DISCUSSION

Aristotle Fallacy: The Fallacy of False Cause

Basic Definition: The general idea of Fallacy of False Cause is that something that can be assumed to be the cause of an event is mistakenly applied as the real cause.

Analysis: In the Officer Misconduct #2 discussion, a student refuses to relinquish her cell phone to her teacher. This results in the teacher calling the school resource officer. After a short verbal exchange with the student, the resource officer uses excessive force and flips the student out of her seat and body slams her to the floor. It is wrongfully assumed by A. White that the reason the student was body slammed was because she refused to give up her cell phone.

A white's blindspot in this instance is in failing to realize that the real cause of why the student was physically assaulted. The real reason was that the school resource officer failed to handle the situation with reasonable force.

BLACK LIVES MATTER DISCUSSION

<u>Aristotle Fallacy</u>: The Fallacy of Many Questions

<u>Basic Definition</u>: The general idea of Fallacy of Many Questions is that a question is asked that has questions within that same question.

<u>Analysis</u>: In the Black Lives Matter discussion, A. White asks A. Black the following question: *Explain why Black Lives Matter only came about when police killed a few black people? How come that group wasn't up in arms because of all the black on black crime that exists?*

A white's blindspot in this instance is in failing to realize that each question has its own set of unique circumstances that may not have a common thread where one can logically link the two questions together with a single answer.

SLAVERY DISCUSSION

<u>Aristotle Fallacy</u>: The Fallacy of False Cause

<u>Basic Definition</u>: The general idea of Fallacy of False Cause is that something that can be assumed to be the cause of an event is mistakenly applied as the real cause.

<u>Analysis</u>: In the slavery discussion, A. White asks A. Black the following question: *How come every time I talk to a black person they ultimately relate all the disadvantages that they have in life back to slavery? Didn't the 13th Amendment fix all this? When will your people take personal responsibility?*

For A. White, the passing of the thirteenth amendment is the main cause of why black people are on equal footing with white people. He believes that the amendment gave black people the opportunity to compete for a better quality of life. However, he failed to realize that Vagrancy laws were implemented along with the thirteenth amendment.

Here is an example of a vagrancy law: If a free black person was unable to prove they had a job, they were fined and put in prison.

The vagrancy laws resulted in the continuation of involuntary servitude and slavery as punishments.

A white's blindspot in this instance is in failing to realize that The thirteenth amendment did not work in isolation and was modified by other laws such as the Vagrancy laws that were in effect at that time and continue into today.

BLUE LIVES MATTER DISCUSSION

Aristotle Fallacy: The Fallacy of Composition

Basic Definition: The general idea of Fallacy of Composition is that something that is true about a part of a group is incorrectly attributed to the whole group without verification.

Analysis: In the Blue Lives Matter discussion, A. White states; "and you guys wonder why we see you as a threat. Trust me when I say that Micah only made the itchy trigger fingers in the police department more sensitive. His actions did not fix the problem."

A. White's blindspot in this instance is apparent when he attributes the mindset of Micah Johnson to all black people. His assertion is the definition of stereotyping and supports bias, prejudice and racism. His assertion may be true about some black people but it does not apply to all black people.

TRUMP DISCUSSION

Applied Fallacy: The Fallacy of Composition

Basic Definition: The general idea of Fallacy of Composition is that something that is true about a part of a group is incorrectly attributed to the whole group without verification.

Analysis: In the Trump discussion, A. White states; "...People are tired of Mexicans who keep coming into the U.S. illegally and abusing our amnesty policies just because they have had children on U.S. land, people are tired of Muslims coming into our country to wait as sleeper cells to blow-up and kill Americans..."

A. White's blindspot in this instance occurs when he fails to realize that only some Mexicans come into America illegally and only some Muslims commit acts of terrorism on American soil. This does not make his statement true for all Mexicans and Muslims.

KAEPERNICK DISCUSSION

Applied Fallacy: The Fallacy of Equivocation

Basic Definition: The general idea of Fallacy of Equivocation is that a word or statement is used repeatedly and with each use, the speaker changes the meaning of the word which creates a misleading or mistaken conclusion.

Analysis: In the Kaepernick discussion, A. white keeps changing the reason why Kaepernick is protesting. In one instance he states "I think people that don't honor the American flag are a disgrace to the United States and should be brought up on treason charges." In another instance he states "But he is disrespecting the country and our military by refusing to stand."

A. White's blindspot occurs when he ignores the real reason why Kaepernick is protesting, which is police brutality, and keeps changing the reason why he believes Kaepernick is protesting. In one instance he states that Kaepernick is disrespecting the flag, in another instance he states that Kaepernick is disrespecting the country and the military. The meaning keeps changing.

WHY AM I BEING DETAINED? DISCUSSION

Applied Fallacy: The Fallacy of False Cause

Basic Definition: The general idea of Fallacy of False Cause is that something that can be assumed to be the cause of an event is mistakenly applied as the real cause.

Analysis: In the Why Am I Being Detained? discussion, A. White states;"...When you are stopped by a police officer he can detain you. Police ask the questions they don't answer questions."

A. White's blindspot in this instance is based upon the premise that the police officer does not have to explain why he detains an individual and that citizens are compelled to comply once he or she has been stopped. Based on most stop and identify statutes in each state an officer who detains an individual has a duty to follow certain procedures during the detention process. Police do not have absolute power as A. White suggests.

THINGS DON'T ADD UP? DISCUSSION

Applied Fallacy: The Fallacy of False Cause

Basic Definition: The general idea of Fallacy of False Cause is that something that can be assumed to be the cause of an event is mistakenly applied as the real cause.

Analysis: In the Things Don't Add Up? discussion, A. White states; "She saw a potential crime in progress and she did the right thing.", and he also states that "It is not like they knew each other and they were having a lover's quarrel that turned violent." These statements in and of themselves are not conclusive in regard to what actually happened.

A. White's blindspot in this instance is based upon the premise that the police officer's explanation of what happened is supported by the circumstances and not necessarily the evidence. A. white's viewpoint has neither been proved nor disproved because all the evidence has not yet been presented to the public as the investigation is ongoing.

REMEMBER ME

Andy Lopez 13

Santa Rosa, CA

Killed; October 22, 2013

Crime: Lopez was Carrying a pellet gun that resembled an AK-47 assault rifle. After officers reportedly told Lopez to drop the gun, he turned toward them and they shot him

Aftermath: No Indictment

5

CODE ICE

*"You look like a f****** bitch in heat, and if you get r*ped by a pack of ni**ers, it will be your fault."*

-Mel Gibson
Actor

On April 16, 1963 a great US civil rights leader named Martin Luther King whose progressive thinking preceded the times in which he lived stated that:

"Injustice anywhere is a threat to justice everywhere."

The Bryce Masters' tragic ordeal makes it crystal clear what Martin Luther King was talking about and makes it evident why everyone, regardless of color, creed or religion must align and make their voices heard when injustice rears its ugly head.

NEGLIGENT USE

Beside the initiation of the Taser, whose success is debatable, law enforcement procedures, processes and protocols have not changed much in 50 years. In fact, if we go back to the Taser which was created in 1974 as an alternative to using a gun, which is a lethal weapon, and take a look at the tasers effectiveness, we will find that the taser has only been moderately successful in saving lives. The main reason this is true is because the Taser can be continuously applied by an officer. This makes it a lethal weapon.

Bryce Masters, a 17 year old white teenager found himself in a very similar position as Sandra Bland on September 14, 2014, the day he was stopped by officer Timothy Runnel of the Independence Missouri police department for reasons still unknown today.

Because of the harrowing experience that Bryce went through, the Masters family on a large scale, could relate to how black people feel when they are faced with excessive force and abuse by law enforcement. In fact, Matt Masters was quoted saying

> *"I get a lot of sympathy from my black cop friends," who have said to him that, "this is what we've been saying about cops for a long, long time!"*[44]

The Bryce Masters' traffic stop was caught on dash cam video. The events that follow, start from the point where Officer Timothy Runnels walks to the driver's side of Bryce's car and knocks on the window, which is partially rolled down.

THE STOP

Officer Runnels	*"Roll it all the way down"*
Bryce	*unintelligible*
Officer Runnels	*"I can't hear you, you have to roll it all the way down"*
Bryce	*"You can't hear me?"*
Officer Runnels	*"Roll it all the way down"*
Bryce	*"I can hear you"*
Officer Runnels	*"Roll it all the way down"*
Bryce	*"For what?"*

At this point Officer Runnels leaves the passenger side of the car and goes to the driver window. As he approaches Bryce can be heard telling the officer that his window won't roll down. After hearing this, Officer Runnels opens the driver's door.

Officer Runnels	*"Get out"*

Bryce	*"For what?"*
Officer Runnels	*"Out now"*
Bryce	*"For what?"*
Officer Runnels	*"Out!"*
Bryce	*"Am I under arrest?"*

Officer Runnels does not answer whether or not Bryce is under arrest and grabs Bryce's arm and pulls him out the car. From this point the two struggle with each other.

Officer Runnels	*"Out!. I am going to pull you out if you don't come out."* Do you really want to get tased right here..?
Bryce	*"For what?"*
Officer Runnels	*"Get your ass out now!"*
Bryce	*"I haven't done anything officer.*
Officer Runnels	*"Give me your hand—you are under arrest."*

Bryce	*"For what?"*

At this point Officer Runnels stops trying to pull Bryce out of the car, steps back and pulls his Taser. Before he fires the taser, the video is at the 1:18 mark and he can be heard saying "All right, fuck it then" and starts firing the taser. When he finally stops firing the Taser, the video is at the 1:41 mark. Bryce was electroshocked with 50,000 volts for a full 23 seconds! During police training, trainers taze trainees with 50,000 volts for no more than 5 to 7 seconds and the trainees have been quoted as saying that the experience is extremely unpleasant.

While Officer Runnels was deploying the taser, Bryce was no longer able to speak. As the taser was firing, Officer Runnels ordered Bryce out of the car by shouting "Out of the car, out of the car,". As he gives this command he grabs Bryce's cell phone from his hand and throws it. Bryce struggles out of the car to get on the ground. When he finally reaches the ground he cries out in excruciating pain "Ahhhhhhh!"

With the Taser still firing, Officer Runnels says "Told ya." He continues firing the Taser and instructs Bryce to put his hands behind his back. At this point in the tape Bryce can be heard making a gurgling sound and is only able to move on the ground slowly in response to the pain. All the while the ticking sound of the Taser can be heard. Finally Officer Runnels stops firing the Taser, puts his knee in Bryce's back and grabs his hands to put on handcuffs. As he is doing this, Bryce is still making the gurgling sound. The officer grabs Bryce by both arms from the back and says "stand up, stand up." Bryce is unable to stand because of the damage inflicted by the Taser, but Officer Runnels proceeds to drag him from the street towards the sidewalk. Officer Runnels then drops Bryce to the ground and Bryce's full dead body weight slams into the concrete. When this happens, Bryce's teeth slam together and several of his teeth break into fragments as his jaw dislocates. With no concern or awareness of the damage he has done to the teen, Officer Runnels begins to frisk Bryce. Bryce can now be heard making low murmuring groans to indicate that he is in pain. This is where the tape ends.

From the time the paramedics arrived on the scene to the arrival of the ambulance at the hospital Bryce was unconscious and had started turning blue.

Medical staff furiously worked to keep him alive. Nurses cut his clothes off and placed ice packs around his body to prevent his brain from swelling. They called for scans and tests. Blood and mucus had crusted around Bryce's nose. His face was swollen, with some dirt and asphalt mashed into his cheek. His chin was split open. His skin was pale, and his lips were light blue. Bryce was showing acute signs of decorticate posturing... His fingers and toes were curled inward, and his arms bent at near 90-degree angles toward his chest. These are classic signs of a brain injury.[44]

As a result of being electroshocked by Officer Runnels with 50,000 taser volts for a full 23 seconds, Bryce's brain had been deprived of oxygen for six to eight minutes. During that time he was in cardiac arrest and incurred brain damage.

A neurologist who worked on Bryce had the unfortunate duty of letting Bryce's parents know that Bryce was in a coma and that his Glasgow Coma Score, which is a way to measure the severity of a brain injury, was a three. Three was the worst score out of a possible high of fifteen.

A three meant that there was only a 50% chance that Bryce would recover from the coma. It also meant that if he was lucky enough to wake up out of the coma that he most likely would not recover beyond a vegetative state.

Based on the grim diagnosis the only chance that Bryce had for survival and recovery was to undergo a procedure called Code ICE — a "therapeutic hypothermia" that slows the blood flow of a coma patient to keep the brain from swelling. Bryce would spend several hours cooling down, this procedure would take a minimum of 24 hours and then he would be slowly warmed back up.

Over the next few days, the medical team that watched over him needed to work overtime to save his life.

Once Code ICE was in process Bryce's mom and dad remained at the hospital. They waited all night into the next morning as Bryce's core body temperature was cooled down to 92.6 degrees – exactly six degrees below normal body temperature. Once this temperature was reached it was a waiting game for the next 24 hours. *"Bryce would be in limbo as his brain tried to heal itself."*[44]

As Bryce fought for his life, his dad and former police officer Matt Masters started investigating exactly what happened during the stop to see if he could understand the circumstances that would explain why his son was lying in a coma. Every step Matt took to uncover the truth was met with allusive explanations by the police department, but being a former cop, Matt knew what was going on and did not like it one bit.

As he looked into his son's case, the first thing he encountered, which his black friends had encountered, was the biased police reports to the media. The police had initiated an explanation for the stop and slanted the story to make Bryce the blame for his own circumstances.

It was clear that officials were determined to place blame on Bryce and paint a picture of a lawful stop that escalated into a justified use of force.

The first news reports about the incident included comments from a spokesperson who said Bryce was stopped for an outstanding warrant, and that he refused to follow the officer's commands. "He was just being completely uncooperative with the officer," the spokesperson told KCTV. Later, a different spokesperson would tell KCTV that "the use of the Taser was in policy." It was clear that officials were determined to place blame on Bryce and paint a picture of a lawful stop that escalated into a justified use of force.[44]

Although Matt was aware that police accounts are not always 100% accurate, he assumed that Bryce had most likely caused the officer to have to use his taser because he believed that police don't forcibly apprehend citizens without cause. It wasn't until he watched the dash-cam video that he saw the horrifying truth of what really happened to Bryce at the traffic stop.

While watching the police dash-cam footage, Matt saw that at the 1:18 mark in the video Officer Runnels can be heard saying "All right, fuck it then" and he deploys his Taser. As Matt watched, his concern turned to horror as he watched Officer Runnels continued to pump Bryce with 50,000 volts of electricity. The Taser was still deployed after 15 seconds. *It was unbearable for Matt to watch. He jumped up from his seat and yelled, "What the fuck? Holy fuck, let off the goddamn trigger!"* [44]

After an investigation, the video fully exonerated Bryce from any wrongdoing. Matt now questioned his assertion that *police don't forcibly apprehend people for nothing.*

> *The video also shook the convictions he had always held about law enforcement officers. "Instead of putting faith in my own son, I put faith in a fellow officer —and that he was a professional. I don't understand how an officer could treat anybody's kid that way."* [44]

The next thing he encountered, was the deliberate falsification of evidence that would be used to help acquit Officer Runnels of any wrongdoing. The main question on the table was why did Bryce get stopped in the first place?

Being a former police officer, Matt was able to get internal department information that the general public could not. Through his contacts he found that the initial search warrant application that Officer Runnels submitted, indicated that Bryce was stopped because there was an outstanding warrant on the plate attached to his automobile. But the department knew this reason would not stand-up in court. The department was aware, just like Matt's mom and dad that Bryce's license was valid and his car had been registered in his mom and dads name for over three years. There was no outstanding warrant—so the department knew that the report had to be changed.

A few days later Matt received information about the new search warrant application. The new reasons listed for Bryce being stopped were that *Officer Runnels "observed the vehicle to have darkly tinted windows," and that after Bryce partially rolled down his window, he "detected an odor of marijuana coming from inside the vehicle."* [44]

Once Matt received information on the report he explained to his contacts what the department was allowing Officer Runnels to do in order to avoid prosecution.

> *"You see what's happening here," Matt told them. "They're working it backwards." Matt's experience as a cop taught him that officers can sometimes write themselves out of trouble through exaggerated and self-serving reports. "Whenever you see these officers come out with a use of force, whether it be a shooting or a Tasering or a whatever, there are phrases that always go in those reports, that we've been trained to put in there," Matt said. "And so many times that's just like an 'insert quote here' in your report because that's going to cover your ass."*

> *Matt saw the phrasing and knew Runnels was looking for ways to justify both the stop and the attempted arrest. Matt suspected that once it was clear the warrant association to the car wasn't sufficient probable cause for an arrest, Runnels needed new justifications. Since smell is subjective, and difficult to prove, officers can use "marijuana odor" broadly to justify probable cause, Matt said. "Cops use that all the time."* [44]

Matt and his family were system scapegoats. It was them against the law enforcement machine—and the machine did not like to lose. Because he was fighting the system Matt's inherited white privilege was 'taken' from him and he and his family were treated in the same manner as black and brown people. Matt will go down in history as one of a few white men in America who actually has a remote idea of what it feels like to be treated like a black man.

Many white people are fortunate enough to never have their 'whiteness' put on trial so they never see the unfair side of the justice system at work. Unfortunately Matt and his family had the unique opportunity to stand on the side of society where only the black and brown people stand. The only major difference is that Matt and his family are white so the treatment they received had nothing to do with racism; it was the result of the corruption and abuse of power that permeates throughout many police departments in America. The thing that still plagued Matt was that as a police officer recruit trainee he had been zapped with a Taser and had seen a dozen "funny" Taser videos of his police trainee colleagues screaming and making funny faces as they were pumped with electricity and not one ended up like his son Bryce. Based on his own experience as a police officer and the training he received as a police officer, Matt was under the impression that a Taser could not kill.

Matt knew Officer Runnels had taken the exact same training that he did. For this reason alone, Matt actually felt sorry for Officer Runnels. The department had lied to them both. Not directly but indirectly. Neither of them was told everything that they needed to know regarding Taser safety. There were two things that Matt was confident about:

> *Runnels may have been a bad cop, but if he hadn't been given a device that Taser International had assured him was extremely unlikely to kill, then he might not have been tempted to shock a teenager who simply wanted to know why he was being arrested.*

> *A police officer is only as good as the training he receives.*[45]

Forty-Eight hours after Bryce started the Code ICE procedure, he miraculously emerged alive from the coma! It was a miracle that the Masters family was blessed with.

With Bryce's life no longer in jeopardy, Matt was determined to learn the truth about Tasers. Matt started by retracing the safety training provided by Taser International

Inc., a company headquartered in Scottsdale, Arizona, that created the Taser and trains police departments on Taser safety measures.

As he researched deaths related to Taser shocks Matt recalled a *syndrome called "excited delirium," which he'd learned about in his Taser training from Taser International. This is the diagnosis given by Taser International when people sometimes died after a Taser shock.*

> *As it happens, the concept of "excited delirium" is highly controversial. Used both as a description of a state of mind as well as a medical diagnosis, excited delirium is a phrase that medical examiners sometimes use in official reports after a person is severely injured or killed in an intense police interaction. It is not recognized by the American Medical Association or the American Psychological Association, nor is it listed in the Diagnostic and Statistical Manual of Mental Disorders. But Taser International has latched onto the diagnosis as a way to explain many deaths that occur after someone has been shocked with a Taser.*

> *One police psychologist accused Taser International of using the "mythical" disorder as a way to justify "ridiculously inappropriate" Taser use by police officers.*[44]

Matt also found that the actual number of Taser related deaths is currently between 500 and 1000 based on the particular reference source.

As Matt's search continued, he mapped out a timeline of events starting in 2004 that contradicted the training that he received from Taser International.

2004

Matt took his initial Taser training and was assured that the weapon's electric current would not cause death.

2006

A Taser safety study by Patrick J. Tchou, a cardiac electrophysiologist at the Cleveland Clinic determined that a Taser shock can potentially lead to cardiac arrest. The study was financed by Taser International.[44]

2007

No mention that a Taser shock can potentially lead to cardiac arrest in police training

2008

No mention that a Taser shock can potentially lead to cardiac arrest in police training

2009

Taser International released a bulletin suggesting that officers should avoid shooting suspects in the chest when possible. According to the company, the preferred target area was changing for reasons that had more to do with the ineffectiveness of chest shots than any danger associated with the potential of cardiac arrest.[44]

2010

No mention that a Taser shock can potentially lead to cardiac arrest in police training

2011

No mention that a Taser shock can potentially lead to cardiac arrest in police training

2012

No mention that that a Taser shock can potentially lead to cardiac arrest in police training

2013

No mention that a Taser shock can potentially lead to cardiac arrest in police training

2014

No mention that a taser shock can potentially lead to cardiac arrest in police training. Bryce Masters was tased across the heart for 23 seconds; he died for 8 minutes, and ended up in a coma.

Once Matt uncovered all the ugly details that contradicted what he had been taught about Taser safety, he felt that police departments across the country had been lied to by Taser International.

> *"It's sickening to me to listen to Taser even speak," Matt continues. "We've all been duped. We've been fooled by a company that has made millions and millions of dollars off of the police departments."*[44]

One thing that Matt did not mention, that absolutely must not be forgotten is that the negligence of taser International and police departments across the country has resulted in about 750 taser involved deaths, since the taser was introduced as a law enforcement weapon.

> *Bryce's eyes began to scan his room inside the intensive care unit. He was completely immobilized.....he was making eye contact with his mom and dad. Single tears began to run down his face, but his pain was a good sign. He wasn't just alive — he was demonstrating awareness.*[44]

Bryce's damage assessment included the following:

His tongue was raw and swollen and several of his teeth were crushed. A few were sheared in half. As his consciousness improved he began to spit out teeth fragments.

His jaw was sore because it had popped out of place. The medical staff popped it back in when he was in the coma.

This traumatic encounter left Bryce with a noticeable limp as he had to drag one leg in order to start walking again.

He ended up with severe short-term memory loss which contributed to bursts of anger and frustration resulting from not being able to remember events. In some cases Bryce was unable to retain memories that were less than 24 hours old.

> When his rehab started, Bryce was given simple tasks, *"things kindergartners could do,"* as he put it. *Drawing shapes, holding objects firmly in his hand, walking without a limp, hearing a story and trying to synopsize it back to the storyteller — things that used to be second nature were now exhausting chores. Most of the damage Bryce suffered, though, was done to his psyche. The memories he had formed over 17 years, many of the things he thought made him who he was, no longer applied.* [44]

In return for his role in what could ultimately be classified as attempted murder, Officer Runnels was indicted on four counts; two related to obstruction of justice and two related to deprivation of rights. One obstruction charge was related to filing a false police report, there was no information on the other obstruction charge. One deprivation of rights charge was related to Officer Runnels' action of continuing to forcibly apprehend Bryce by keeping his Taser deployed when Bryce was no longer a threat. The other deprivation of rights charge was related to dropping Bryce face first on the ground when he was already restrained.

CREDENTIALS OVERSIGHT

In the aftermath of some of these police shootings it has been found that some officers contained information in their personnel Files that may have disqualified them from being hired by a police department.

For example, in the case of Tamir Rice, Officer Loehmann recklessly broke standard apprehension protocol and ended up killing twelve-year-old Tamir Rice. Officer Loehmann had been deemed unfit to serve by his previous employer but this information was not discovered or ignored during the application process and the officer was hired onto the Cleveland police force. The exact same thing happened in the Bryce Masters case. Officer Runnels had resigned from his previous employer, the Kansas City police department, under threat of termination before transferring into the Missouri Independence Police department.

The following incident was noted: During roll call one day, Runnels was describing a recent unsuccessful hunting trip. During the otherwise unobjectionable story, Runnels said he and his friends decided to switch tactics and try "ni**er hunting" instead. Word spread quickly in the unit about the foul-mouthed cop who was written up on the spot for nonchalantly using a racial slur during a gathering of officers. The story became notorious among Kansas City cops. [44]

After witnessing this egregious behavior, why would a police department that wanted professional officers, and who knew what it truly meant to protect and serve, re-hire someone with this attitude and state of mind? Even though Bryce's case is not one that stems from racial insensitivities it still reflects how an officer's perspective, attitude, and approach to policing can lead to poor judgment, poor critical thinking and poor decision making. All of which lead to harmful and deadly outcomes for citizens.

REMEMBER ME

Oscar Grant, 22

Oakland, CA

Killed; January 1, 2009

Crime: Shot in the back by Bay Area Rapid Transit (BART) Officer Johannes Mehserle after being forced to lie face down on a train platform

Aftermath: Officer Mehserle found guilty of involuntary manslaughter and was released under parole after serving eleven months. BART settled Grant's daughter and mother for 2.8 million in 2011.

OSCAR IS WHY BLACK LIVES NEED TO MATTER

Photo Courtesy of Yahoo!

Bryce's horrific, life-threatening encounter came about because of a simple traffic stop---a basic, non-criminal, non-threatening traffic stop! A warning should have been issued then the officer and suspect should have been on their way. But this did not happen. As long as police procedures and protocols are not monitored and enforced, innocent victims will continue to be hurt or killed. The list below is a testament of this assertion:

Rumain Brisbon	Dontre Hamilton	Botham Jean
Alberta Spruill	Deion Fludd	Ervin Jefferson
Dante Parker	Wendell Allen	Tamon Robinson
Tyree Woodson	Kajieme Powell	Prince Jones
Tyre King	Rekia Boyd	Victor Steen
Victor White III	Jerame Reid	Raheim Brown
Yvette Smith	Jordan Baker	Timothy Stansbury

..and countless others

It is time to implement changes and new ideas to protect our citizens. We can no longer stand by afraid to disrupt the status quo within the ranks of law enforcement. It is time for some changes. In this section we will explore some ideas that if implemented could make the risk of harm to both police officers and citizens who unintentionally break the law—low, while keeping the risk of harm for criminals who deliberately break the law—low as well, relative to the circumstances.

LAW ENFORCEMENT REFORM

Observation of the current law enforcement procedures and protocols will reveal that the system is highly slanted to make sure criminals cannot slip through procedural loopholes. This is great! However, there is one major problem; the same system is used to apprehend individuals who commit misdemeanors. Police have no idea who is a hardened criminal or law abiding citizen who commits a misdemeanor so they apprehend individuals at one intensity – Maximum impact! This means that individuals who commit misdemeanors and those who perpetrate horrible crimes are viewed equally and have the same risk of losing their lives.

GOD COMPLEX REFORM

A basic change that could be made that might save lives is to make it mandatory for officers to tell citizens whom are being apprehended exactly why they are being arrested. This is an essential point of de-escalation that could prevent any unnecessary confusion or frustration which could lead to a violent or deadly police altercation.

This small change would have prevented tragedies like the Sandra Bland death, the Eric Garner killing and the near death of Bryce Masters. All three individuals were non-threatening and only wanted to know why they were being apprehended before allowing the officers to arrest them. In all three of these cases they were never told why they were being apprehended. The officers initiated what I call the GOD complex. They decided that they were the almighty, all powerful, to a fault. They deprived the citizens of their right to know exactly what they had done. In many cases where the police refuse to disclose the reason for the traffic stop, they are buying themselves time while they dredge up other evidence that can be used as alternate reasons for an arrest. This very unethical tactic needs to be stopped. Federal legislation should be passed that makes it mandatory for officers to give a clear, well-defined response when an individual who is being apprehended asks why they have been detained or are being arrested.

TECHNOLOGY REFORM

Police who obey the law and have nothing to hide are probably thankful for dash cams and body cams which record traffic stops. Corrupt officers who go through their career waiting to make someone's life a living hell, hate these new systems which hold them accountable for their actions. They have found ways to "outsmart" the technology by doing simple things such as moving a suspect out of the field of view of the recording dash cams or conveniently forgetting to turn on their body cams. With today's technology there are easy ways to mitigate intentional sabotage of the safety systems put in place to protect both officers and civilians.

One way to mitigate intentional sabotage of the safety systems would be to throw out broken tail light traffic stops including subsequently found evidence for stops that have no dash cam or body cam video to support the officer's claim.

Equal Force Mandate

Gun owners cannot just shoot the first person that mouths-off or kill someone when they get pissed without dealing with the consequences. In both cases mentioned, the gun owner would most likely be faced with multiple charges that will unequivocally include excessive force. Why should this be any different for our law abiding police officers. They too should be held responsible for making sure that they use the proper amount of force to apprehend citizens in all cases.

We have all seen the videos where the suspect is already handcuffed and on the ground with three officers on top of him. At this point the individual poses no threat, yet from somewhere off screen an officer feverishly runs into the scene and jumps on top of the pile of officers. This type of behavior serves no purpose except to injure or kill the allegedly guilty party at the bottom of the pack. An equal force mandate would help to regulate excessive force and help to change the law enforcement culture so that officers will not abuse their power and are held accountable.

MY COMMUNITY, MY RESPONSIBILITY INITIATIVE (MMI)

When officers are disconnected from the communities they serve, the officer and citizens of that community are put at risk. The officer has no idea who the people are who have a disability, who have a medical condition, who live in the area and who does not. Imagine how effective and efficient law enforcement could be when addressing the issue of crime if police departments built relationships with the citizens they serve. Officer Tommy Norman (discussed in chapter 3) has proven that there are benefits to community policing.

Before a cadet graduates from the police academy he should be required to do three to six months of community service in the primary community that he or she will patrol. This requirement would give the police candidate an opportunity to build relationships with people in his community on a personal level. This would also allow him to establish trust with community members.

Part of the MMI initiative should also include a six month ride along as an EMT assistant because individuals who have the capability to take life should also know how to save life.

REMEMBER ME

Stephon Clark, 22

Sacramento, CA

Killed; March 18, 2018

Crime: Mistaken for another suspect that was reportedly breaking car windows. When confronted by the police officers in his grandmother's backyard, his cellphone was mistaken for a gun and he was shot at twenty times with eight shots hitting him in the back.

Aftermath: An investigation is pending and the officer's names have been withheld.

STEPHON IS WHY BLACK LIVES NEED TO MATTER

Photo Courtesy of Yahoo!

FEDERAL LAW ENFORCEMENT TRAINING REFORM

The idea of this reform is to enact a Federal Police Certification process that will ensure high standards of ethics and best practices across police jurisdictions. After going through the Federal certification process, an officer could go to their home station and get specialized training that may only apply to their jurisdiction. The benefit of implementing this change is to implement best practices and a code of ethics that extends across police departments throughout the country. This common core training will reveal itself through consistency of how the law is enforced, regardless of jurisdiction.

A simple example of standard training has existed in the military for decades. Every person in the military must attend Basic Military Training School (BMTS) before their military career can begin. Training facilities are located in specific areas of the country and every trainee receives standardized training. Specialized training begins when they arrive at their home office. If the military uses this process, why would it be any different for law enforcement, which is a paramilitary agency.

Today, police training for cadets takes about 19 weeks and consists of physical, mental and procedural training and basic law classes. An individual who decides that this is his or her career of choice will be entrusted to uphold the American constitution and laws for all U.S citizens. They will also be given the power to enforce the law and take life. Things don't get more serious than this so it is critical to impose procedural standardization and consistency.

The impact of standardized training would cause a dramatic change in the police culture. Cadets who take this training would essentially "speak the same language" as other cadets from different areas of the country because of common training. In addition to this, police would operate with much more consistency and citizen's would be safer. Each police officer would now have a common code of conduct and consequences as jurisdictional training would have to be in line with federal training.

PROPER PROCEDURES FOR APPREHENDING A MENTALLY ILL SUSPECT

Another way of combating racism and abuse is by removing the police officer's ability to legally justify improper and questionable actions especially as it relates to the use of deadly force by a police officer.

One case in point regarding proper procedures is the unlawful killing of Tanisha Anderson. In a fifty-eight page Justice Department Report, it was found that Cleveland police officers were not properly trained to handle individuals like Tanisha Anderson who suffer from mental illness. In this case the officers were not properly trained to use de-escalation techniques and they wound up using excessive force. One officer, using his full body weight kept his knee in Ms. Anderson's back as she lay face-down on the pavement while getting handcuffed. As a result of this forceful apprehension Ms. Anderson died. Her official cause of death was ruled "sudden death associated with physical restraint in a prone position,"[12] according to the medical examiner's office.

As discussed in the Tanisha Anderson case, when police officers are not properly trained to apply de-escalation techniques when dealing with medically or mentally ill citizens, the risk that a suspect will either take flight or put up a fight increases and is escalated.

Mentally ill people may reflexively take flight or fight in moments of stress or if they are cornered and their personal space is restricted. Law enforcement officers need to be trained how to determine when a situation has escalated to a point where a suspect's natural response is to take flight or fight, and they should understand how to appropriately apply de-escalation techniques. Both actual and perceived threats to a suspect can trigger either type of response.

When police attempt to apprehend mentally ill citizens without communicating why, the fight or flight response can be activated based upon the mentally ill person's state of mind at the time. When police withhold information it can produces anxiety and fear in the person being apprehended. Even in situations where the individual is innocent, the fight or flight response is set to engage. This feeling is no different than the feeling you get when you are sitting at a traffic light and look into your rear view mirror and see a police cruiser behind you. Even if you have done nothing wrong, your heart may begin to beat just a little faster.

PROPER PROCEDURES TO PREVENT PERSONAL INTEREST

When an officer has a personal interest in the outcome of an interaction with a civilian, he breaks standard procedure and knowingly escalates a situation by using language that is insulting or condescending. When this personal interest exists the officer will do whatever he can in order to solicit a reaction from a suspect he is apprehending whether or not the person is mentally ill, medically ill or compliant.

The Sandra Bland case is an example of an officer who had a personal interest in her apprehension because she was not intimidated by his presence. Because his ego was insulted he found a reason to escalate the situation.

The exchange below occurred after a traffic stop and Officer Encinia is clearly trying to escalate the situation into something more

Officer Encinia	"You Ok?"
Ms. Bland	"I'm waiting on you. This is your job."
Officer Encinia	"You seem irritated."
Ms. Bland	"I am, I really am. You were tailing me so I move over and you stop me, so yes I am irritated."

Officer Encinia	"Are you done?"
Ms. Bland	"You asked me what was wrong and I told you, so yes I am done now."
Officer Encinia	"Put out your cigarette please."
Ms. Bland	"I'm in my car I don't have to put out my cigarette."
Officer Encinia	"Well you can step out now."
Ms. Bland	"I don't have to step out of my car... why do I have to step out?"
Officer Encinia	"Ma'am step out that car or I will remove you."

Enforcing proper procedures for apprehending mentally ill citizens and addressing the improper actions of police officers who knowingly escalate a situation by using language that is insulting or condescending, can be achieved by creating a unified set of laws and proper procedures that:

1. Clearly define the actions that are improper

2. Outline the immediate consequences for performing those actions

SMART GUNS

As mentioned in chapter 2, sensor technology could be used to protect the officer and assailants. Guns that have sensor technology would work similar to how smartphones work. Smart phones have an option to unlock when reading a fingerprint. Gun sensor technology would work the same. When the officer grabs his weapon sensors would read the print of any finger touching the gun. If the fingerprint does not match the pre-programmed fingerprint ID, the gun will not fire. This technology would protect an officer in the event he is overpowered and his gun is taken away.

MULTICULTURAL DIVERSE TEAMS

It is a known fact that multicultural diverse teams produce the best outcomes. One example of a good outcome using a diverse team occurred on an episode of Law and Order.

In this particular episode a male officer, Detective Goren and a female officer, Detective Eames, were investigating a crime scene where a woman had been murdered. The woman was found dead sitting on the toilet in a bathroom and her purse was on the floor at the bathroom entrance. Detective Goren started to verbally walk through the crime scene as he explained to his partner Detective Eames how the murder occurred. Here was his account of what happened:

"She came into the bathroom, put her purse on the ground, went over to sit on the toilet and that is when the killer snuck up on her and hit her over the head with a large, heavy object."

As soon as Detective Eames heard his account, she said it did not happen that way. Detective Goren who was visibly confused, replied, "What do you mean it did not happen that way." Detective Eames stated "because women don't put their purses on the bathroom floor!" Without having a diverse team, this information would have been overlooked and the killer may have gotten away or it may have taken longer to catch him.

The main benefit of multicultural teams is that each member of the team can bring a unique viewpoint to each situation. This shared pool of unique information most likely will save lives.

FEDERAL LAW ENFORCEMENT REVIEW BOARD (FLERB)

The idea of a Federal Law Enforcement Review Board is related to the same objective and purpose as the Food and Drug Administration (FDA). In the United States, certain industries are regulated with the primary intent of keeping individuals safe. For example the FDA governs pharmaceuticals, medical products, food industries and more. The FDA provides oversight for each of these industries to make sure the items produced are safe. The FLERB could be an extension of the FDA that specifically deals with reviewing Law Enforcement agencies to make sure they are adhering to a list of defined standards. This unbiased agency would essentially hold the Mayor, Police Commissioner and Precinct leaders accountable for the quality of law enforcement they provide to their community. This board is different from the Attorney General's Office at the white house because it would be proactive. Most times when the Attorney General or special prosecutor get involved with a police related investigation, it is usually too late and an injustice has already been committed and someone is most likely already dead.

As with the FDA and industries that are regulated, if a precinct fails an inspection, there should be an opportunity to address any deficiencies and immediate consequences for failing to address any deficiencies within a federally defined time period.

USE OF UNARMED DRONES

It might sound futuristic but the use of unarmed mini-drones should be allowed to help apprehend individuals. Imagine a mini-drone flying and recording video outside an alleged suspect's car while the officer, in the safety of his car, gives basic commands to the occupants. The camera imagery of the drone could be used as the first check to clear the suspect as a threat. If this option was available a little more than six months ago, Philando Castile would most likely be alive today.

In the Philando Castile incident the police officer would have still been in his car and would have received video and audio from the flying drone to verify Mr. Castiles' information. With the information received, the officer would have been able to clear Mr. Castile as a law abiding gun owner instead of panicking and shooting him.

6

BLUE LAW

"Well, what I would really like is a bunch of little n***ers to wear long-sleeve white shirts, black shorts, and black bow ties. You know, in the Shirley Temple days, they used to tap dance around. Now, that would be a true Southern wedding, wouldn't it?"[1]

-Paula Deen
American Celebrity Chef

From the day the African first set foot on the American continent as a slave, racism and the tools to implement racism were put into full force and effect. The tools of oppression that were to be used to control slaves are articulated in a speech given on December 25, 1712 on the banks of the James River in the colony of Virginia. This speech known as the Willie Lynch Letter was given by a British West Indies slave owner named Willie Lynch as part of a master plan to keep blacks enslaved. It contains several steps in the process of how to make a slave. This letter delineates the four basic steps that are used to keep slaves subjugated. --Hate, Fear, Murder and Language.

At its core, the Willie Lynch Letter instructed slave owners to inflict the psychology of hate, fear, murder, and language to reinforce a self-perpetuating cycle of subjugation and bondage that affected and enslaved all who are held within its grasp. The Willie Lynch letter was an instrument used to transition slavery into modern day racism.

RACISM

Racism is defined as a belief or doctrine in which the inherent differences among human beings determines cultural or individual achievement. Usually this involves the idea that one's own race is superior to another's and that as the superior race one has the right to dominate the other group that is deemed inferior. It is in the implementation of this dangerous and misguided belief that one's race has the right to dominate others, that is at the root cause of the atrocities that we have witnessed in the past and are continuing to witness at an alarming rate today.

Today, the tools of racism; hate, fear, murder, and language, are still in effect, but have only been institutionalized and have become further entrenched and hidden within present day society. The most egregious display of today's racism is present in many police forces and court systems across the United States, attributing to the current mass incarceration problem, which in turn has served to keep black people economically deprived and controlled.

SUBJUGATION AND CONTROL

The steps documented in the Willie Lynch letter were used as an outline to implement subjugation and control through the manipulation of slaves.

The first documented step instructed the slave owner to exploit the differences that exist among the slaves and to use those differences to create a never-ending cycle of HATE or distrust to create division within the slave community and environment.

The second documented step was to create a sense of dependency through FEAR thereby eroding the bond of trust between the female and male slave. This occurs by training the female slave to displace her dependency from the male slave onto the slave owner. This dependency on the slave master renders the male slave powerless against the master. This places the female in an emotional and physical state where she does not believe she can be protected against abuse or violence and must rely solely on protection from the slave owner.

The third documented step was to insert the constant threat of violence and MURDER into the consciousness of the male slave. The threat of violence and actual MURDER directed towards the male slave was used to reshape and redefine the relationship that the female slave had with her male and female offspring. *"For fear of the young male's life she will psychologically train him to be mentally weak and dependent, but physically strong."* [2]

The fourth documented step was to control the LANGUAGE. By destroying the language of the slave (native tongue) and defining the use of language by the slave (native tongue is outlawed, can only speak english), you have an additional layer of control that makes it difficult for the slave to define and maintain a sense of his or her historical origins and values.

FEAR AND HATE: THE ANALYSIS

Subjugation and control as outlined in the Willie Lynch letter was enforced through fear and hate and is used in the present day in many forms; including unjustified police killings; police corruption and abuse of power; and the implementation of unjust laws. In the not too distant past, during the middle to late 1900's, the use of fear and terror was supported by a corrupt police force. One example of a tool used to terrorize black people during this time was the burning of the cross. The burning of a cross in front of the home of a black family was usually a warning or a signal that someone was about to be taken out of their home to be killed. The police supported these crimes because even if they knew these crimes were going to be perpetrated, they would stand by and do nothing.

Today the police support this same fear and terror, not by cross burnings, but by abuse of power and corruption tactics. One modern day example of how police use corruption to terrorize black communities involves, Police Chief Ray Atesiano from the Biscayne Park police department in Miami, Florida. Officer Atesiano instructed officers Raul Fernandez and Charlie Dayoub to pin crimes on innocent black people in order to bolster successful conviction rates. Under his orders, anyone with a record became a target for which unsolved burglaries and other crimes could be pinned on, in order to clean up the books.

"If they have burglaries that are open cases that are not solved yet, if you see anybody black walking through our streets and they have somewhat of a record, arrest them so we can pin them for all the burglaries," one cop, Anthony De La Torre, said in an internal probe ordered in 2014. "They were basically doing this to have a 100% clearance rate for the city." [3]

Chief Atesiano's command to pin crimes on innocent black people resulted with black citizens in the Biscayne Park community where this took place, to be harassed and stopped for bogus charges like burglary.

"The former police chief and two officers in Biscayne Park face federal charges of framing a 16-year-old in four unsolved burglaries. The motivation, prosecutors charged Monday, was keeping a perfect score on crime statistics." [4]

"The arrest reports are sketchy by any measure, listing no witnesses, fingerprint evidence, confessions or even property stolen. Instead, the reports used the same vague language — that the "investigation revealed" T.D. employed the same "M.O." and the homes had a "rear door pried open."[3]

Fear and hate, is also present when an innocent citizen is killed by police or is wrongfully imprisoned. This unlawful and unjustified killing and punishment of human beings is a shameful part of America's past that continues into the present. This is especially true with the killing of men, women, children, the elderly and mentally ill by police officers who are often acquitted. It doesn't stop there. Police are also victims of fear and hate. This fear and hate is an extension of the subjugation and control that is being enforced upon black citizens. It happens in the form of harassment when good police officers break the blue code of silence.

The blue code of silence is used by police officers to continue the Fear and Hate campaign and supports subjugation and control by obstructing and undermining justice. The worst part about it is that the blue code of silence is enforced at multiple levels of our justice system. Examples of this were discussed in chapter three where officer Billy Crystal tried to do the right thing, and reported his fellow detectives for officer misconduct. For being a good cop, he was harassed by his peers, his captain, and he was told to forget what he saw by the Assistant State Attorney. He was also told to forget about what he had seen when he reported the incident to his sergeant. His sergeant also told him to make sure that internal affairs did not find out. In addition to this, he was shunned by superior officers. The final disgrace he was subjected to was that the president of the fraternal order of police refused to assist him in getting justice for the victim of the police misconduct.

REMEMBER ME

Chavis Carter, 21

Jonesboro, AR

Killed; July 29, 2012

Crime: Arrested for an outstanding warrant. He was searched twice, handcuffed with his hands behind his back and placed inside a police patrol car. Found minutes later with a gunshot wound to the head and a gun near his body.

Aftermath: After an investigation his death was ruled a suicide by the Arkansas crime lab.

CHAVIS IS WHY BLACK LIVES NEED TO MATTER

LANGUAGE AND MURDER: THE ANALYSIS

Subjugation and control as outlined in the Willie Lynch letter was enforced through language and murder. During slavery, Slaves codes, which were state laws, were used as tools to protect the supremacy of the slave owner. Slave codes allowed violence to be directed towards slaves as well as people of color with impunity and were set up to justify the legal murder of slaves as well as people of color.

Two such laws are listed below:

SLAVE CODE ENTRY: VIRGINIA, 1705

"And if any slave resist his master, or owner, or other person, by his or her order, correcting such slave, and shall happen to be killed in such correction, it shall not be accounted felony; but the master, owner, and every such other persons giving correction, shall be free and acquit of all punishment and accusation for the same, as if such incident had never happened: and also, if any negro, mulatto, or Indian, bond or free, shall at any time, lift his or her hand, in opposition against any christian, not being negro, mulatto, or Indian, he or she so offending shall, for every such offence, proved by the oath of the party, receive on his or her bare back, thirty lashes, well laid on; cognizable by a justice of the peace for that county wherein such offence shall be committed." [5]

SLAVE CODE ENTRY: LOUISIANA, 1724

"The slave who, having struck his master, his mistress, or the husband of his mistress, or their children, shall have produced a bruise, or the shedding of blood in the face, shall suffer capital punishment." [6]

Whites often punished slaves publicly during the period the slave codes were implemented in order to set an example. One such recorded example of this brutal and barbaric use of the slave code was described by a man named Harding who described the fate of a woman unfortunate enough to get caught in assisting several men in a minor rebellion. "She was hoisted up by her thumbs, whipped and slashed with knives before other slaves until she died."[7]

For an example of the lingering effect of the slave codes, you need look no further than the lynching of Thomas Shipp and Abram Smith on August 7, 1930, which was discussed in chapter two. The murder of Thomas Shipp and Abram Smith is also an example of how the language of the law at the time supported the use of deadly force without consequence. In the present, the language of the law still allows human error, bad judgment, incomprehensible mistakes, and intentional malice by police officers to be justified. The mechanism of how this happens is as follows: A case is appealed to the US Supreme Court - The highest court in the country. If the case is accepted, it is heard and a decision is rendered. The decision that is rendered must be accepted and implemented by the lower level courts, which are the state level courts. This means that the US Supreme Court sets the federal standard for an issue and the state courts, interpret and implement that standard for their state. This is where the trouble occurs. The states are given the autonomy to interpret and implement the federal standard based on their own objectivity.

As it applies to a police officer's use of force, the Supreme Court set standards that allowed each state the leeway to meet the standard without making provisions for the safety of citizens or the intent or motivation of police officers. Here is how this was done:

"In the 1980's a pair of Supreme Court decisions - Tennessee v. Garner and Graham. v. Connor set up a framework for determining when ......[the use of] force by cops is reasonable." [8]

TENNESSEE V. GARNER: A CASE STUDY FOR DEADLY FORCE

In the Tennessee v. Garner case that was heard by the Supreme Court, a father filed a lawsuit against a police officer who killed his son using *deadly force*. His son was unarmed, not a threat, and was fleeing. The lower level details of the case are not important. However, the Supreme Court decision and the interpretation of the decision by the states is. This will be analyzed to show why police abuse remains to be ungoverned.

In this case, the Supreme court ruled that deadly force may only be used to apprehend someone if an officer "reasonably" believes that he or others are at risk of serious physical injury or death.

The ruling set by the Supreme court in this case established an objective standard that the states had to meet regarding the use of deadly force, however, many states implemented laws that met the federal standard without considering language to help alleviate the loss of life caused by accident, mischance, and error in human judgment. The states were able to do this because of the freedom they are given to interpret the word "reasonably."

GRAHAM V. CONNOR: A CASE STUDY FOR EXCESSIVE FORCE

In the Graham v. Connor case that was heard by the Supreme Court, a diabetic who was driving to a convenience store to purchase orange juice filed a lawsuit against a police officer for the injuries he sustained when police used excessive force to detain him.

In this case, the Supreme court ruled that the use of excessive force, whether deadly or not, for the purposes of depriving a citizen of liberty is properly analyzed under the fourth amendment "reasonableness standard". In short, the fourth amendment reasonableness standard covers the idea that deadly force may only be used to apprehend someone if an officer "reasonably" believes that he or others are at risk of serious physical injury or death. Because of this ruling, no new standard was set. This meant the states did not have to make any changes to its' laws to protect citizens from the use of excessive force.

The rulings set by the Supreme court decisions in the Tennessee v. Garner and Graham v. Connor cases established an objective reasonableness standard for determining the level of force that police officers are able to use and an objective standard for determining when deadly force can be used. These rulings still left citizens in danger of being hurt or killed. What the Supreme Court should have done was set a new clearly defined standard that would have forced the states to include a subjective analysis as part of a step by step process to avoid accident, mischance, human error, as well as consider an officer's intent and motivation in order to create laws that meet the standard.

A review of the Alton Sterling case shows what can happen when the law does not have a reasonableness standard that takes into account an officer's underlying intent or motivation.

In chapter 2, Alton Sterling, a 37 year-old African American man was killed while selling CD's when he was shot at close range during a struggle with a police officer. He was reportedly trying to access a gun that he was carrying, to assault a Baton Rouge police officer during the scuffle. One of the officers yelled out "He's got a gun! He's got a gun!...He is going for the gun!" After a few seconds three gun shots can be heard and the video goes black.

Today the actual charges against Mr. Sterling are unknown and it is still not clear whether or not Mr. Sterling had a gun and whether he was carrying it legally in the state of Louisiana which has some of the most lax gun laws in the country.

The general sentiment of many individuals who watched the Alton Sterling apprehension was that he was unjustifiably murdered and that the police who murdered him were racist.

Based on the video evidence, if this was a case where two law abiding citizens had an argument, the citizen who would have killed Mr. Sterling would be going on trial for murder. However, when it comes to police and the way the current laws are written to support the fourth amendment, Police can use deadly force under the veil of racism without worry of consequences. As long as this is the case, the lives of law abiding citizens will be at risk.

"The Fourth Amendment "reasonableness" inquiry is whether the officers' actions are "objectively reasonable" in light of the facts and circumstances confronting them, without regard to their underlying intent or motivation." [9]

To substantiate that the use of force is a critical issue, work is being done at the legislative level in California to change the "Reasonableness Standard" to a "Necessity/Necessary Standard" in order to make it a reality. This standard will be used as a template for other states to emulate.

In California, though, cops in similar situations could soon find themselves subject to a new legal standard -- the strictest in the country. If passed, it could provide a model for other progressive states that have followed California's lead on other issues, including immigration and the environment. [10]

"The bill says lethal force should only be used when it's necessary, and that necessity is only when the public or an officer is in imminent danger. If an officer [or member of the public] is not about to be hurt, officers should use other [de-escalation] strategies," such as verbal warnings, tasers and pepper spray, says Weber.* [10]

Police Officers, Police Chiefs, Commissioners, and Mayors must all be held to a higher standard of accountability. Laws, rules and regulations, procedures and codes of conduct along with mandated training must begin to clearly define in a clear, consistent, and unbiased manner in regard to what a police officer shall and shall not do when interacting with civilians along with adequate penalties for breaking rules.

Change can only begin when the root cause of the problem is acknowledged and a conscious effort is made to bring about the change.

We must never forget that in a growing and evolving society the laws must change to reflect its current circumstances, to balance the use of deadly force in protecting the public, to deter crime, and to prevent the loss of life--citizens and law enforcement.

REMEMBER ME

Ezell Ford 25

Florence, CA

August 11, 2014

Crime: Caught in the crossfire of two police officers.

Aftermath: The Los Angeles Board of Police Commissioners concluded that one officer was justified and one officer violated the rights of Ezell and acted outside of police policy, but neither was charged in connection with the shooting. The City of Los Angeles settled a wrongful death lawsuit brought by the family in October 2016 for 1.5 million.

EZELL IS WHY BLACK LIVES NEED TO MATTER

Photo Courtesy of Yahoo!

HISTORY OF THE POLICE FORCE AND REFORM

It seems like a rhetorical question to ask but it needs to be asked anyway; "Why do we need a police force?" To answer this question a look at the history and development of the police force in America is in order.

North and South

According to Dr. Gary Potter; in his essays-The History of Policing in the United States parts one through six he talks about the history of policing in the United States.

The growth and development of the police force in America as we find it today has its genesis in both the northern and southern states of America.

In the northern states the system of policing consisted of volunteers that were complemented by paid enforcement officers. In the southern states the system of policing consisted of those individuals who controlled the slave population in that part of the country. This group was known as The Slave Patrol. This role consisted of apprehending runaway slaves; creating terror to deter revolts; and executing summary justice outside of the law for any violation of plantation rules.

In both the northern and southern states, crime was defined by the actions of the underclass.

In the north, public drunkenness, political protest, alcohol and drug distribution, worker riots, gambling, prostitution, and gangs just to name a few, defined criminal behavior.

In the southern states, criminal behavior was defined in two phases. The first phase was before the Civil War where runaway slaves and slave revolts defined criminal behavior. The second phase occurred shortly after the Civil War and was defined by controlling freed slaves.

Both systems functioned and evolved along the lines of controlling the underclass populations. This was done based upon weighing economic interests against the need to control crime while maintaining social order into the present day.

As the foundation of policing continued to grow, the language of the law served two very important purposes:

The first purpose was to deter criminal behavior where written law was supplemented by a police force that was on the ready to enforce it. This infrastructure coupled with upper class greed provided the scaffolding to support a stable and disciplined workforce after the Emancipation Proclamation, which granted freedom to slaves in Confederate states, on New Year's Day in 1863. The stable workforce was a result of the upper class control of the financial and economic resources, which left the underclass in a state of economic dependence. The underclass were forced to stay as part of the work force and work under deplorable conditions. Their other option was to resort to criminal behavior and end up in jail as police enforced the law. This in turn led to convict leasing which left the underclass working for little to no wages while keeping the workforce mechanism in full swing. This corruption and unfair treatment of the underclass was all supported by the language of the law.

The second purpose was to define punishment that would be administered for criminal behavior. Establishing this infrastructure allowed an upper class influenced police force to focus on the illegal actions of individuals or specific groups as defined by the language of the law. This allowed the business-minded upper class to shift the focus away from social and economic conditions that they created in order to maintain a never ending cycle of poverty and deprivation. This corruption was all supported by the language of the law.

The overall intent of the language of the laws in both the northern and southern states served to give power and authority to the police officer's shield and uniform while simultaneously giving justification for the gun, nightstick and use of paramilitary tactics by the police officer. The power and authority given to the police officer in turn, supported political corruption and provided a stronghold for continued economic exploitation and political abuses. The unprecedented levels of exploitation and abuse along with organized crime brought with it a need for law enforcement reform.

STAGES OF LAW ENFORCEMENT REFORM

The powers to be made several efforts to initiate law enforcement reform to fix the issues that were created by the language of the law, but all efforts failed. Throughout history law enforcement reform had gone through four stages; Commissions, Internal Restructuring, Professionalism and Community Policing.

The first stage of police reform: Commissions can be review boards and investigatory agencies who temporarily formed groups that challenge the police force. The goal of the commision reform was to put independent groups in place who could request changes in internal procedures and processes within the police force. With regard to the language of the law and how it allowed corruption to continue within the police force, commissions failed to fix the problem. The main reasons they failed was because commissions functioned as a temporary body and they only had the ability to make recommendations but they did not have the ability to influence the direction of the police department.

The second stage of police reform: Internal restructuring occurs when an agency is internally reorganized. The goal of internal restructuring reform was to sever the police function from political control or influence. The reason why this reform was unsuccessful was because the change that was implemented created smaller compartmentalized units within police units. Each function now operated independently within the department. The traffic unit, criminal investigation, vice and narcotics units all were siloed. Making this change actually made it easier for organized crime groups and political entities to influence corruption within the police department because with the smaller groups, they had less people to deal with.

The third stage of police reform: Professionalism is defined by performing tasks while following a strict set of principles and procedures. The goal of professionalism reform was to improve police effectiveness and to reform policing as an institution by placing an emphasis on military style organization and discipline. The reason why this reform was unsuccessful was because like internal restructuring, professionalism not only operated within a bureaucracy but had the effect of damaging relationships within respective communities where police were meant to serve because civilians were subjected to military style police tactics. These tactics were viewed by communities as repressive. The police now represented dictatorship and control instead of protecting and serving the people within the community.

The fourth stage of police reform: Community policing is a law enforcement program in which police officers often working on foot, bicycle, or horseback are assigned to specific neighborhoods or communities to work with residents in preventing crime. The central goal of community policing is for police to build relationships within communities by creating partnerships and implementing strategies so they can work with residents to reduce and prevent crime. Additionally there are two secondary goals; the first is to give police more autonomy to make decisions, and the second is to provide a means to make citizens feel more comfortable with what is being done to address the problem of crime in their respective communities.

With respect to the first secondary goal of autonomy to make decisions beyond how criminals are apprehended and how arrests are made, a police officer is powerless and has no impact. Decisions to make real economic and climate change in a community must be made by his superiors.

With respect to the second secondary goal of making citizens feel more comfortable with what is being done to address the problem of crime in their respective communities, police like Officer Tommy Norman of the Arkansas Police Department are making this a reality.

Even though community policing provides some positive benefits based on its central goal of building relationships within communities for the purpose of reducing crime, research concludes that community policing has no meaningful impact in this area.

"There are three reasons why police have virtually no impact on crime as it relates to community policing." [11]

First, police officers cannot and do not prevent crime. Police facilitate the apprehension of individuals suspected of committing criminal behavior and they also assist in the gathering of evidence that proves the suspect to be guilty of said crimes.

Second, "Community policing requires placing decision making and discretion in the hands of police officers." [11]

If decision making was put into the hands of the police officer, it would create a dilemma. The dilemma would occur between the police officer and the community citizen because even though the officer would be trying to create meaningful partnerships within the community he would still have to enforce the law. It would not be unrealistic to believe that the officer may need to lock up the same citizen who yesterday viewed him as a friend and ally. This dilemma undermines the strategy of creating meaningful partnerships that could benefit the community, because it divides the community and makes the police officer appear to be a person that you can trust on one hand, and someone you cannot trust on the other.

*Third, "there is no universally accepted criteria for evaluating the
success or failure of community policing."* [11]

In order to measure the success or failure of community
policing, specific goals would need to be set and measured.
Achieving these goals would require participation at every
level from street-level officers up through police
supervisors, law enforcement executives, and the entire
community. This infrastructure is currently not in place
due to the time and cost factors involved. The police force is
a quasi-military force that distributes power and authority
based upon a hierarchy that is resistant to delegating
authority to its lower level members. Second, developing a
partnership with members of any community requires time;
time for the police officers to understand the social and
economic needs of that community; time to develop a
cultural sensitivity that fosters a willingness of community
members to embrace a police-community relationship; time
for change within respective police departments to be
implemented. Because these changes represent continuous
improvement, police officers would in essence be working
themselves out of a job.

Based upon the Northern and Southern division in
America, the Use of Law, and failed Police reform you now
have additional insight of why the history of policing in
America is a deplorable, shameful and disgraceful one.
America has selfishly used the police officer as an
instrument of power to perpetuate racism.

POWER, RACISM, AND SOCIAL CONTROL

When one has the power to legally take another person's
life, they can make life and death decisions. When malice
and bad intent are added to the power that these
individuals possess, we end up seeing certain groups of
people who suffer as a result. In this section we will analyze
the different types of power by showing how they can be
utilized to achieve dominance and how they in effect
support racism.

According to Robert S. Feldman, there are six types of power.

Reward Power – The ability to give rewards when others comply with your wishes.

Coercive Power – The ability to deliver punishments.

Referent Power – An example of a type of behavior or thinking that others may or may not want to emulate.

Legitimate Power – When a position or role defines an individual's level of power.

Expert Power – When expertise and knowledge is the source of and individual's power.

Informational Power – When power is grounded in what is known about the content of a specific situation.

The Police Officer is one of the few unique individuals who can access each type of power based upon how they choose to interact with other individuals.

To understand how power is abused in order to perpetuate racism, we will analyze several case studies that use a combination of the six types of power identified by Robert S. Feldman.

CASE STUDIES FOR POWER AND RACISM

Milgram

According to Stanley Milgram, power granted by one's job can serve to perpetuate racism and abuse.

With respect to police officers being used to maintain an atmosphere of racism and abuse, our first analysis of a case study done by Milgram focuses on the consequences of being obedient to authority. This case study serves as an example of how a police officer's unquestioning obedience to laws and how the power granted to an officer by his job can serve to perpetuate racism and abuse. We define this as Legitimate Power.

While it can be argued that racism is not the intent of our laws, the reality is that the furtherance of racism and abuse is the final outcome when police enforce the law in many instances. In Milgram's experiment that we will discuss, teachers and learners were used to prove this point. The teachers in his experiment represented the authority figure who has Expert Power to steer and manipulate the learner.

In Milgram's experiment, teachers were instructed to give electrical shocks to learners when questions were answered incorrectly. Teachers were also instructed to treat silence as an incorrect answer and to increase the electrical shock intensity given to the student. In the experiment, the students were not given actual electrical shocks but the teacher was not made aware of this. This is a form of Coercive Power in that the teacher delivered a form of punishment for either an incorrect answer or being non responsive. Milgram also demanded the teacher to deliver a shock to the learner even when hesitant about doing so. From this experiment, Milgram learned three very significant things about teachers being compliant when pressured to proceed.

The first thing he learned was that a teacher was more likely to continue with the experiment when the authoritative figure was in close proximity.

The second thing he learned was that teachers were more likely to continue with the experiment when they could pass on responsibility for any injury caused by the electrical shocks to the learners or experimenter.

The third thing he learned was that teachers were more likely to proceed with the experiment if they believed that a respected organization sponsored it.

Superimposing this idea of obedience to authority and replacing the role of the teacher with that of a police officer and replacing the role of student with a civilian, Milgram's experiment shows why the role of a police officer who does not have proper guidelines can lead to the perpetuation of abuse and racism.

REMEMBER ME

Ramarley Graham 18

Bronx, NY

February 2, 2012

Crime: Being in the wrong place at the wrong time. Ramarley was shot in the bathroom of his apartment because the officer thought Ramarley had a gun based upon conversations he heard on his police radio. A bag of marijuana was found near him but no gun.

Aftermath: The officer who shot Ramarley had his manslaughter conviction thrown out and was not reindicted. In January of 2015 the City of New York agreed to pay 3.9 million to the family of Ramarley Graham.

RAMARLEY IS WHY BLACK LIVES NEED TO MATTER

ZIMBARDO

Our second case study of how racism can be perpetuated, focuses on an experiment called the Stanford Prison experiment that was conducted by Phillip Zimbardo. This experiment highlights how the justification of abuse or racism can be disseminated throughout an organization based upon the morals and values of a person in a position of authority and his relationship with his subordinates.

In the Stanford Prison experiment there was a group of individuals who were divided into two groups. One group was identified as Prisoners and the second group was identified as Guards. Zimbardo represented the prison superintendent and his research assistant represented the warden. The Guards in this experiment were given the authority by Zimbardo to use psychological techniques and strategies to break down the individuality of the Prisoners in order to create a sense of powerlessness.

The experiment was initially scheduled to last for two weeks but was discontinued after six days because the players in the experiment began to take on the real identities of the roles they were playing. The Guards became psychologically and physically abusive towards the Prisoners. The prisoners took on real prisoner traits and characteristics where some prisoners actively accepted psychological abuse, other prisoners began to harass other prisoners at the request of guards, and some prisoners harassed other prisoners who were trying to stop the abuse.

The experiment got out of control because similar to the individuals who played the prisoner role, Zimbardo began to take on the traits of his role as prison superintendent and no longer was operating from his role as the research psychologist. As a result, he created a sense of powerlessness within the prisoner population. This unforeseen change biased his interest in the outcome of the experiment. Because of this he allowed unethical acts to be performed under his supervision and allowed the valuable results that could have been gained from this experiment to outweigh the risk of physical and psychological harm to the participants.

One important point that can be drawn from Zimbardo's experiment is that he lost focus of his true role and no longer cared about the welfare of the people in the experiment. This behavior is no different from when police officers lose focus of the oath they took to protect and serve when they interact with civilians and become reckless with the safety of civilians. When an officer loses focus like this because of the power he possesses and is motivated by racism, his interest in the outcome of apprehending a suspect will many times outweigh the risk of physical and psychological harm to civilians.

An example that shows what can happen when the interest in the outcome of an arrest outweighs the risk of physical and psychological harm that can be done is the Bryce Masters case that was discussed in chapter five. Here is a recap.

Bryce Masters, a 17 year old white teen was stopped for a minor automobile infraction. The arresting officer never told him what he was being stopped for and was so adamant about arresting him that the officer tased Bryce across the heart for 23 seconds. This was unnecessarily done to make an arrest during a traffic stop for an unknown charge. During this ordeal Bryce died for 8 minutes, ended up in a coma and barely survived his life threatening injuries.

Just as in the Zimbardo experiment, this officer was so fixated on making an arrest that he gave no thought about the risk of physical harm that would result from his actions.

Once the Zimbardo experiment concluded, it was determined by the American Psychological Association that rules needed to be implemented to preclude any harmful treatment to participants of future experiments. Based on this discovery, the implementation of ethical guidelines for police officers should be established as a first step in combating the racism and police abuse that is inherent within the hierarchical relationship that exists between civilians and law enforcement.

SOCIAL CONTROL

With respect to police officers being used to maintain an atmosphere of racism and abuse, the remaining theories focus on social control and socialization.

According to Sociology professor Ashley Crossman, social controls are norms, rules, laws, physical organization of society, and institutions within society that can serve to guide how we interact with others. Family, religion, education, media, law, politics, and the economy are examples of societal institutions. These institutions can provide guidance on what to think, as well as how to interact with others.

There are two types of Social control--Formal and Informal.

Formal Social Control refers to those laws, rules and codes of conduct that are produced and enforced by the government and/or its representatives.

Informal Social Control refers to those values and beliefs that we learn through the process of socialization.

According to the article written by Nicki Lisa Cole, Ph.D., socioeconomic status produces a hierarchy whereby ones' status determines the opportunities, rights, and obligations that one has amongst others. Status also creates racial boundaries as well.

According to Michelle Alexander author of The New Jim Crow, *the first step in erecting and maintaining the boundaries that socioeconomic status creates through racism, is to grant law enforcement officials extraordinary discretion regarding whom to stop, search, arrest, and charge..., thus ensuring that conscious and unconscious racial beliefs and stereotypes will be given free reign."*
[13]

An example of a law enforcement officer abusing his discretion to stop a citizen without proper justification occurred when Aramis Ayala (Florida's first minority state attorney) was stopped on June 19th, 2017.

During what appeared to be a normal traffic stop, Ayala was pulled over. An officer approached her and she gave him an ID. This was their verbal exchange once he received the ID:

Officer	*"What agency are you with."*
State Attorney Ayala	*"I'm a state attorney."*
Officer	*"Thank you, your tag did not come back, I've never seen that before. That was the reason for the stop."*
State Attorney Ayala	*"What was the tag run for?"*
Officer	*"We run tags all the time whether it's at traffic lights and that sort of stuff. That's how we figure out if cars are stolen and that sort of thing. Also the windows are really dark. I don't have a tint measure but that's another reason for the stop."*
State Attorney Ayala	*"Do you guys have cards?"*

There are two concerns with this stop that give rise to questions. The first question was why was she stopped in the first place; and the second question was, how can a police officer determine if tinted windows are illegal without a tint measure?

The officer stated that his run of the plate which returned no information was the reason for the stop. If nothing came back upon a check of her license plates then she should not have been stopped because police officers know that *state-issued vehicles are confidential, and would not come back as registered to a vehicle*.[14]

For this part of the incident the broad definition of the law allowed the officer to make a stop even though his license plate check showed that the plates were confidential. This occurred for no other reason than the officers personal bias. This is the only plausible reason because all officers know that state-issued vehicles are confidential and have confidential plates.

The officer also stated that he thought the window tinting was too dark. However, he admitted that he did not have a tint measure. How can this be considered a legitimate reason to stop someone if the officer does not have the tools required to make a proper assessment?

For this second part of the incident, the law allowed the officer to make a stop based upon his subjective judgment. When he could not support his falsely applied judgment about the tinted windows, he used his knowledge of the law to try and explain away an abuse of his discretion as he did not have a tint measure to justify his second reason for stopping her.

Overall, this was an unwarranted and unjustified stop and the officer used his knowledge of the law and the broad leeway he is given by the language of the law, to try and explain away an abuse of his discretion to implement his own form of social control.

CALHOUN

To further review forms of social control we will review social interaction within a space that limits access to resources and opportunities by analyzing an experiment done by John B. Calhoun. Calhoun's experiment was done with rats who initially were given all the basic essentials with one exception; they were not given space to accommodate an increase in the population. With an increase in population, the rat community had a breakdown in the ability to continue to co-exist harmoniously during this experiment. Increases in the population caused dominate males to become aggressive and subordinate rats to withdraw. As a result of the limited space and increased social interaction there was a breakdown and reassignment of complex social behaviors such as aggression and conflict resolution. The change in aggression and complex social behaviors due to increased social interaction has a human correlation. The equivalent human behavior occurs when the social interaction between humans increases. If the social interactions increase in the presence of unequal power, the outcome can lead to violence and an abuse of power as seen between police officers and black civilians.

For example, the shooting death of an unarmed Philando Castile as discussed in chapter two is a clear example of how the risk of injury to a civilian is increased by continuous confrontations with a police officer. In the Philando Castile case, Mr. Castile had been previously stopped by the police fifty-two times for various traffic violations. On his fifty-third stop he was killed.

REMEMBER ME

Steven Eugene Washington, 27

Los Angeles CA

Killed; March 20, 2010

Crime: Being autistic and reaching for his cell phone in his waistband.

Aftermath: In May 2012, his mother received a $950,000 settlement.

STEVEN IS WHY BLACK LIVES NEED TO MATTER

BLACK WALL STREET

In his 1967 transcribed speech; *The Three Evils Of Society*, (See Appendix) Martin Luther King Jr. talks about the second societal evil of excessive materialism. Excessive materialism is a form of poverty. If two groups are competing for limited resources and one group has greater access to these resources, the other group will now be subjected to a form of social control due to a lack of access. This lack of access will keep one group impoverished.

Poverty in any form can be devastating for any group of people to endure. However, when it is combined with social control and racism against black people and is supported by laws and law enforcement, it creates a culture that supports the economic and social suppression of black people.

An example of economic and social suppression is the Tulsa Race Massacre. The Tulsa Race Massacre was an attack that occurred from May 31, 1921 through June 1, of 1921. The attack was carried out on the ground and by air and destroyed more than 35 blocks of the wealthiest black community in the U.S., which was located in the Greenwood district of Tulsa, Oklahoma. This community was referred to as the *Negro Wall Street*, which is now known as *The Black Wall Street*.

Black Wall Street found its humble beginnings in 1899 when J.B. Stradford, a black entrepreneur who believed that economic progress for blacks could be achieved through the pooling of resources and by working together and supporting each other's businesses. The large tracts of land that he purchased were only sold to other blacks.

In 1906, O.W. Gurley, another entrepreneur, took a leadership role in implementing collective economics by purchasing 40 acres of land from J.B. Stradford that he used for the development of several businesses.

By 1910 the Black Wall Street area in Tulsa, Oklahoma, was booming with black business. The success of Black

Wall Street was a combination of thriving black-owned businesses and also the fact that several prominent black businessmen were homeowners who lived in the area.

Racial segregation laws helped black owned business in the Greenwood district to be successful. These racial segregation laws restricted blacks to only doing business with other blacks. This kept the money circulating within the black community.

The demise of the Black Wall Street started on May 31, 1921 when a black male shoe shiner named Dick Rowland was accused of an alleged assault of a white female elevator operator. During this time it was a common occurrence that black people who were accused of perpetrating crimes against white people were snatched out of their prison cell by an angry mob to get lynched. To preempt such an occurrence, after Dick Rowland was taken into custody by the police, a group of armed black men came to where he was being held to prevent him from being lynched.

The lynching of Dick Rowland was stopped because of a confrontation between armed black men and a group of white men at the police station where he was being held. The gun battle that ensued left several people dead. As news of the killings of both blacks and whites spread throughout the city, violence erupted.

Mobs of angry whites ransacked and torched several blocks of homes and businesses in the Greenwood area. The Black Wall Street business owners and families in the area were unable to defend themselves because the city government had joined the massacre and sided with the whites under the guise of protecting the city against a Negro uprising. The City Police force also sided with the whites and used airplanes to drop firebombs on buildings, homes, and fleeing families.

The aftermath of this massacre left about ten thousand black people homeless, with an estimated total amount of thirty-one million dollars worth of damage in real estate and personal property by today's standards. Almost immediately after the massacre ended, a team of businessmen formed a council and the efforts to restore Black Wall Street began. But the damage was too great and the community never fully recovered.

This is another example of how racism and law enforcement can be used to maintain social control over a group of people.

THE WOLF PACK

And finally, our last social theory looks at racism and abuse as an integral part of a social structure from the perspective of the wolf pack. As pointed out in chapter two, the role and contribution that each wolf makes is dependent upon his or her ranking. Each role is defined by dominance and aggression and not necessarily size. With respect to the omega wolf, The role of the omega is one of submission to the aggression of the other wolves who rank higher within the hierarchy. The role of the omega is to help in maintaining the pack structure through providing an outlet for aggression without dominance or rank within the hierarchy being challenged. As a result of socioeconomic control, human beings also live within a hierarchy where the omega wolf can be considered to be your average citizen.

But unlike wolves whose order within the hierarchy is more firmly fixed by laws of nature and the interplay of aggression, dominance, and submission, human beings have the ability to question aggression, dominance, and submission. Further, human beings also have the ability to give voice to questions of morality, especially as it relates to the role of the police officer and his/her interaction with civilians.

In the wolf pack, the role of the omega is by no means static and there is opportunity for movement up through the hierarchy if submission is replaced by aggression and recognized dominance. This reversal of aggression while rarely seen by the omega wolf in the wolf community is seen most clearly in the case of the civilian known as Micah Johnson.

Just as there are those who believe that the actions of Micah Johnson were wrong and that there was no rational justification for his actions, there are those who believe that his actions and words were not the ranting and ravings of just an angry black man. There was logic to his actions.

By viewing the actions of Micah Johnson within the context that violence leads to more violence, and that sometimes what appears to be an injustice is required in order to restore a respect for justice, his actions can then be viewed and compared to the actions of Nat Turner in his fight to overthrow oppression during slavery. If the actions of Nat Turner are looked at as being a spiritual awakening, then the actions of Nat Turner just like the actions of Micah Johnson hint at a logic where an act of violence is used to express one's moral beliefs. In the case of Micah Johnson, he expressed his moral beliefs through an act of violence in order to shed light on and give voice to questions about the unlawful killing of black people by police. This viewpoint is further supported by a quote made by Thomas Jefferson; *"From time to time the tree of liberty must ... be watered with the blood of Tyrants and Patriots...."*[15]

Many times when the violent actions of an individual are simply placed into a category of being good or bad, or right or wrong, we unknowingly absolve ourselves of the obligation and responsibility of asking why the violence occurred in the first place. With respect to Micah Johnson we know his actions were a direct result of racism, abuse and social control over black people.

REMEMBER ME

Aiyana Jones, 7

Detroit, MI

Killed: May 16, 2010

Crime: Jones was shot when a Special Response Team raided the duplex she lived in. Officers threw a grenade into Jones' apartment. Officer Joseph Weekly claimed Jones's grandmother grabbed his gun, causing Jones to be shot.

Aftermath: Weekly was charged with involuntary manslaughter. His first trial ended in a mistrial. So did his second.

AIYANA IS WHY BLACK LIVES NEED TO MATTER

7

WE THE PEOPLE

Every conclusion, inference and quote in this book has a purpose and is significantly related to the overall theme of the story you've just read, even though at first glance it may not appear to.

For example, each chapter starts with a quote from a Hollywood actor, a television personality or someone with political influence. And each quote was steeped with racist overtones. The significance in doing this is to show that racism is present in every aspect of our society and that it has very influential platforms that can perpetuate its existence and continuance. In fact, in this day and age the look, taste and smell of racism has completely diffused into the most powerful and influential public office in America— The White House.

The Donald Trump story is well known so there is no need to elaborate, however, this gives you a very good idea of just how much marketing and branding that racism has in our society. It also shows that as a country, we are not afraid to use it as a tool for whatever purpose we need to achieve.

Now that you've read this story, you see that racist police officers and certain parts of the legal system are not the only individuals who perpetuate racist views, racist attitudes and death throughout the black community. The well-known, influential people of Hollywood, Television and Politics are also front and center and support this campaign. One might say that the group of Hollywood constituents is not as dangerous as racist police and corrupt legal system, but my question would be this: What is more dangerous, the fire burning the wood or the fuel that is being poured on the fire that keeps the wood burning? Hollywood, Television and Political constituents represent the latter. If they are using the language and not denouncing it as reprehensible they are one source of fuel that keeps racism as a burning platform in our society.

Black Panther Party member Eldridge Cleaver is quoted saying "There is no more neutrality in the world. You either have to be part of the solution, or you're going to be part of the problem."

Hollywood, Television personalities, Political leaders—Take Note!

BLACK LIVES DO MATTER

You have undoubtedly noticed how every ten or so pages we highlighted an innocent black life that was taken with no regard or remorse. In this book we highlighted less than forty lives that were taken, however, in 2012 approximately four-hundred innocent black lives were taken. Everything is disturbing about these deaths, but even more disturbing is the fact that the infrastructure of our capitalistic society is supposed to be governed by agencies who protect people.

The Federal Aviation Agency (FAA) does inspections to make sure the corporate airlines are properly following the rules to make sure lives are not in jeopardy. The Food and Drug Administration (FDA) inspects companies who sell drugs, medical products, etc.... to make sure medical industry procedures are not putting lives in danger. The law enforcement industry relies on internal affairs, the police review board, and when it calls for it, an independent police commission to investigate affairs of the police.

If the FAA suspects wrongdoing by an airline company the company can be shut down, a medical company who is not being diligent and following federal policy can be shut down, but for some reason a police department with questionable ethics and overtones of racism never gets shut down. In most cases they are investigated, problems are discovered, but the problems are not corrected.

Most of this book centered around how racism is the basis of many problems in America's history and how it continues to be a problem in America.

The problem of racism is summed up eloquently by Martin Luther King is his 1967 Transcribed Speech: The Three Evils of Society that was mentioned in chapter six. In his speech he states;

"True compassion is more than flinging a coin to a beggar, it understands that an edifice which produces beggars, needs restructuring." [1]

The police officer like the edifice of racism is a reflection of the morals and values of our society. The police officers' gun, his badge, his oath, and his actions have taken on a life of its own within a system of institutionalized racism.

The police officer has remained an instrument that is used in America to perpetuate racism. If we reflect back to Dr. King's quote, the officer represents a human being without compassion, and black citizens represent the beggars. When the police officer flings the coin of "reasonable force" at a black citizen, all are left poorer. The police officer is left poorer because he loses value and credibility when he does his job and feels as though he does not need to give consideration to the necessity of his actions. In essence he remains morally bankrupt. The beggar becomes poorer because he loses even more value and is left with a two-sided coin in his casket. One side reflects the face of a slain victim. The other side reflects the value that has been placed upon that human life.

As a whole, the institution of racism must be torn down. One place we can start is by restructuring the duties and obligations of the police officer. His job must be shaped so that he places a much higher value on the preservation of ALL human life when apprehending suspects and addressing crime and disorder.

The competencies of a police officer need to be defined by merit, ethics training, and clear circumstances under which deadly force can be used.

Additional requirements of being a police officer should be that he needs to take a more supportive role in helping communities articulate problems, concerns, and issues. This will help each community define and resolve its own problems. Once this is done, the community can then leverage financial and political resources to make change.

CHANGE BEGINS WITH YOU!

ABOUT THE AUTHORs

M. Triplett and H. Triplett

M. Triplett and H. Triplett are both Mentors, Authors, Tutors, and Humanitarians, and they have authored two books together. Their autobiography Perforated Fiber, and their controversial novel on police brutality—The Good The Bad and The Blue. Their novel Perforated Fiber is the basis for their Survival Metaphysics program and is required reading at Springfield Technical Community College in Springfield Massachusetts. This novel The Good The Bad and The Blue will be used to keep issues of police brutality at the forefront of conversation. M. Triplett and H. Triplett are working with college professors and hope to make The Good The Bad and The Blue required reading for criminal justice, psychology and sociology courses. The goal of writing The Good The Bad and The Blue was to inspire politicians, lawmakers and law enforcement agencies to find solutions to the ongoing police brutality issues in America.

M. Triplett and H. Triplett are available to speak about their novels and to conduct At-risk youth workshops. You can contact them at the email address below.

Contact: communityeducationaloutreach1@gmail.com

APPENDIX

WILLIE LYNCH LETTER

The Willie Lynch Letter: The Making of a Slave! This speech was delivered by Willie Lynch on the bank of the James River in the colony of Virginia in 1712. Lynch was a British slave owner in the West Indies. He was invited to the colony of Virginia in 1712 to teach his methods to slave owners there. The term "lynching" is derived from his last   name.

December 25, 1712

Gentlemen:
I greet you here on the bank of the James River in the year of our Lord one thousand seven hundred and twelve. First, I shall thank you, the gentlemen of the Colony of Virginia, for bringing me here. I am here to help you solve some of your problems with slaves. Your invitation reached me on my modest plantation in the West Indies, where I have experimented with some of the newest and still the oldest methods for control of slaves. Ancient Rome's would envy us if my program is implemented. As our boat sailed south on the James River, named for our illustrious King, whose version of the Bible we cherish, I saw enough to know that your problem is not unique. While Rome used cords of wood as crosses for standing human bodies along its highways in great numbers, you are here using the tree and the rope on occasions. I caught the whiff of a dead slave hanging from a tree, a couple miles back. You are not only losing valuable stock by hangings, you are having uprisings, and slaves are running away, your crops are sometimes left in the fields too long for maximum profit, you suffer occasional fires, and your animals are killed. Gentlemen, you know what your problems are; I do not need to elaborate. I am not here to enumerate your problems; I am here to introduce you to a method of solving them. In my bag here, I have a foolproof method for controlling your black slaves. I guarantee every one of you

that if installed correctly it will control the slaves for at least 300 years [2012]. My method is simple. Any member of your family or your overseer can use it. I have outlined a number of differences among the slaves and make the differences bigger. I use fear, distrust and envy for control. These methods have worked on my modest plantation in the West Indies and it will work throughout the South. Take this simple little list of differences and think about them. On top of my list is "age" but it's there only because it starts with an "A." The second is "COLOR" or shade, there is intelligence, size, sex, size of plantations and status on plantations,attitude of owners, whether the slaves live in the valley, on a hill, East, West, North, South, have fine hair, coarse hair, or is tall or short. Now that you have a list of differences, I shall give you an outline of action, but before that, I shall assure you that distrust is stronger than trust and envy stronger than adulation, respect or admiration. The Black slaves after receiving this indoctrination shall carry on and will become self-refueling and self-generating for hundreds of years, maybe thousands. Don't forget you must pitch the old black Male vs. the young black Male, and the young black Male against the old black male. You must use the dark skin slaves vs. the light skin slaves, and the light skin slaves vs. the dark skin slaves. You must use the female vs. the male. And the male vs. the female. You must also have you white servants and overseers distrust all Blacks. It is necessary that your slaves trust and depend on us. They must love, respect and trust only us. Gentlemen, these kits are your keys to control. Use them. Have your wives and children use them, never miss an opportunity. If used intensely for one year, the slaves themselves will remain perpetually distrustful of each other.

Thank you gentlemen,

Let's Make a Slave

It was the interest and business of slaveholders to study

human nature, and the slave nature in particular, with a view to practical results. I and many of them attained astonishing proficiency in this direction. They had to deal not with earth, wood and stone, but with men and by every regard they had for their own safety and prosperity they needed to know the material on which they were to work. Conscious of the injustice and wrong they were every hour perpetuating and knowing what they themselves would do. Were they the victims of such wrongs? They were constantly looking for the first signs of the dreaded retribution. They watched, therefore with skilled and practiced eyes, and learned to read with great accuracy, the state of mind and heart of the slave, through his sable face. Unusual sobriety, apparent abstractions, sullenness and indifference indeed, any mood out of the common was afforded ground for suspicion and inquiry. Let us make a slave. What do we need? First of all, we need a black nigger man, a pregnant nigger woman and her baby nigger boy. Second, we will use the same basic principle that we use in breaking a horse, combined with some more sustaining factors. What we do with horses is that we break them from one form of life to another that is we reduce them from their natural state in nature. Whereas nature provides them with the natural capacity to take care of their offspring, we break that natural string of independence from them and thereby create a dependency status, so that we may be able to get from them useful production for our business and pleasure.

Cardinal Principles for Making a Negro

For fear that our future Generations may not understand the principles of breaking both of the beast together, the nigger and the horse. We understand that short range planning economics results in periodic economic chaos; so that to avoid turmoil in the economy, it requires us to have breadth and depth in long range comprehensive planning, articulating both skill sharp perceptions. We lay down the following principles for long range comprehensive economic planning. Both horse and niggers is no good to the economy in the wild or natural state. Both must be broken and tied together for orderly production. For orderly future, special and particular attention must be paid to the female and the youngest offspring. Both must be crossbred to produce a variety and division of labor. Both must be taught to respond to a peculiar new language. Psychological and physical instruction of containment must be created for both. We hold the six cardinal principles as truth to be self-evident, based upon the following the discourse concerning the economics of breaking and tying the horse and the nigger together, all inclusive of the six principles laid down about. NOTE: Neither principle alone will suffice for good economics. All principles must be employed for orderly good of the nation. Accordingly, both a wild horse and a wild or nature nigger is dangerous even if captured, for they will have the tendency to seek their customary freedom, and in doing so, might kill you in your sleep. You cannot rest. They sleep while you are awake, and are awake while you are asleep. They are dangerous near the family house and it requires too much labor to watch them away from the house. Above all, you cannot get them to work in this natural state. Hence both the horse and the nigger must be broken; that is breaking them from one form of mental life to another. Keep the body take the mind! In other words, break the will to resist. Now the breaking process is the same for both the horse and the nigger, only slightly varying in degrees. But as we said before, there is an art in long range economic planning. You must keep your eye and thoughts on the female and the offspring of the horse and the nigger. A brief discourse in offspring development will shed light on the key to sound economic principles. Pay little attention to the generation of original breaking, but concentrate on future generations. Therefore, if you break the female mother, she will break the offspring in its early years of development and when the offspring is old enough to work, she will deliver it up to you, for her normal female protective tendencies will have been lost in the original breaking process. For example, take the case of the wild stud horse, a female horse and an already infant horse and compare the breaking process with two captured nigger males in their natural state, a pregnant nigger woman with her infant offspring. Take the stud horse, break him for limited containment. Completely break the female horse until she becomes very gentle, whereas you or anybody can ride her in her comfort. Breed the mare and the stud until you have the desired offspring. Then you can turn the stud to freedom until you need him again. Train the female horse whereby she will eat out of your hand, and she will in turn train the infant horse to eat out of your hand also. When it comes to breaking the uncivilized nigger, use the same process, but vary the degree and step up the pressure, so as to do a complete reversal of the mind. Take the meanest and most restless nigger, strip him of his clothes in front of the remaining male niggers, the female, and the nigger infant, tar and feather him, tie each leg to a different horse faced in opposite directions, set him afire and beat both horses to pull him apart in front of the remaining nigger. The next step is to take a bull whip and beat the remaining nigger male to the point of death, in front of the female and the infant. Don't kill him, but put the fear of God in him, for he can be useful for future breeding.

The Breaking Process of the African Woman

Take the female and run a series of tests on her to see if she will submit to your desires willingly. Test her in every way, because she is the most important factor for good economics. If she shows any sign of resistance in submitting completely to your will, do not hesitate to use the bullwhip on her to extract that last bit of resistance out of her. Take care not to kill her, for in doing so, you spoil good economics. When in complete submission, she will train her offsprings in the early years to submit to labor when they become of age. Understanding is the best thing. Therefore, we shall go deeper into this area of the subject matter concerning what we have produced here in this breaking process of the female nigger. We have reversed the relationship in her natural uncivilized state she would have a strong dependency on the uncivilized nigger male, and she would have a limited protective tendency toward her independent male offspring and would raise male offsprings to be dependent like her. Nature had provided for this type of balance. We reversed nature by burning and pulling a civilized nigger apart and bull whipping the other to the point of death, all in her presence. By her being left alone, unprotected, with the male image destroyed, the ordeal caused her to move from her psychological dependent state to a frozen independent state. In this frozen psychological state of independence, she will raise her male and female offspring in reversed roles. For fear of the young males life she will psychologically train him to be mentally weak and dependent, but physically strong. Because she has become psychologically independent, she will train her female offsprings to be psychological independent. What have you got? You've got the nigger women out front and the nigger man behind and scared. This is a perfect situation of sound sleep and economic. Before the breaking process, we had to be alertly on guard at all times. Now we can sleep soundly, for out of frozen fear his woman stands guard for us. He cannot get past her early slave molding process. He is a good tool, now ready to be tied to the horse at a tender age. By the time a nigger boy reaches the age of sixteen, he is soundly broken in and ready for a long life of sound and efficient work and the reproduction of a unit of good labor force. Continually through the breaking of uncivilized savage nigger, by throwing the nigger female savage into a frozen psychological state of independence, by killing of the protective male image, and by creating a submissive dependent mind of the nigger male slave, we have created an orbiting cycle that turns on its own axis forever, unless a phenomenon occurs and re-shifts the position of the male and female slaves. We show what we mean by example. Take the case of the two economic slave units and examine them closely.

The Nigger Marriage

We breed two nigger males with two nigger females. Then we take the nigger males away from them and keep them moving and working. Say one nigger female bears a nigger female and the other bears a nigger male. Both nigger females being without influence of the nigger male image, frozen with an independent psychology, will raise their offspring into reverse positions. The one with the female offspring will teach her to be like herself, independent and negotiable (we negotiate with her, through her, by her, we negotiate her at will). The one with the nigger male offspring, she being frozen with a subconscious fear for his life, will raise him to be mentally dependent and weak, but physically strong, in other words, body over mind. Now in a few years when these two offspring's become fertile for early reproduction we will mate and breed them and continue the cycle. That is good, sound, and long range comprehensive planning.

Warning: Possible Interloping Negatives

Earlier we talked about the non-economic good of the horse and the nigger in their wild or natural state; we talked out the principle of breaking and tying them together for orderly production. Furthermore, we talked about paying particular attention to the female savage and her offspring for orderly future planning, then more recently we stated that, by reversing the positions of the male and female savages, we created an orbiting cycle that turns on its own axis forever unless a phenomenon occurred and resift and positions of the male and female savages. Our experts warned us about the possibility of this phenomenon occurring, for they say that the mind has a strong drive to correct and re correct itself over a period of time if I can touch some substantial original historical base, and they advised us that the best way to deal with the phenomenon is to shave off the brute's mental history and create a multiplicity of phenomena of illusions, so that each illusion will twirl in its own orbit, something similar to floating balls in a vacuum. This creation of multiplicity of phenomena of illusions entails the principle of crossbreeding the nigger and the horse as we stated above, the purpose of which is to create a diversified division of labor thereby creating different levels of labor and different values of illusion at each connecting level of labor. The results of which is the severance of the points of original beginnings for each sphere illusion. Since we feel that the subject matter may get more complicated as we proceed in laying down our economic plan concerning the purpose, reason and effect of crossbreeding horses and nigger, we shall lay down the following definition terms for future generations. Orbiting cycle means a thing turning in a given path. Axis means upon which or around which a body turns. Phenomenon means something beyond ordinary conception and inspires awe and wonder. Multiplicity means a great number. Sphere means a globe. Cross breeding a horse means taking a horse and breeding it with an ass and you get a dumb backward ass long headed mule that is not reproductive nor productive by itself. Crossbreeding niggers mean taking so many drops of good white blood and putting them into as many nigger women as possible, varying the drops by the various tone that you want, and then letting them breed with each other until another cycle of color appears as you desire. What this means is this; Put the niggers and the horse in a breeding pot, mix some assess and some good white blood and what do you get? You got a multiplicity of colors of ass backward, unusual niggers, running, tied to a backward ass long headed mule, the one productive of itself, the other sterile. (The one constant, the other dying, we keep the nigger constant for we may replace the mules for another tool) both mule and nigger tied to each other, neither knowing where the other came from and neither productive for itself, nor without each other.

Control the Language

Crossbreeding completed, for further severance from their original beginning, we must completely annihilate the mother tongue of both the new nigger and the new mule and institute a new language that involves the new life's work of both. You know language is a peculiar institution. It leads to the heart of a people. The more a foreigner knows about the language of another country the more he is able to move through all levels of that society. Therefore, if the foreigner is an enemy of the country, to the extent that he knows the body of the language, to that extent is the country vulnerable to attack or invasion of a foreign culture. For example, if you take a slave, if you teach him all about your language, he will know all your secrets, and he is then no more a slave, for you can't fool him any longer. For example, if you told a slave that he must perform in getting out "our crops" and he knows the language well, he would know that "our crops" didn't mean "our crops" and the slavery system would break down, for he would relate on the basis of what "our crops" really meant. So you have to be careful in setting up the new language for the slaves would soon be in your house, talking to you "man to man" and that is death to our economic system. In addition, the definitions of words or terms are only a minute part of the process. Values are created and transported by communication through the body of the language. A total society has many interconnected value systems. All the values in the society have bridges of language to connect them for orderly working in the society. But for these language bridges, these many value systems would sharply clash and cause internal strife or civil war, the degree of the conflict being determined by the magnitude of the issues or relative opposing strength in whatever form. For example, if you put a slave in a hog pen and train him to live there and incorporate in him to value it as a way of life completely, the biggest problem you would have out of him is that he would worry you about provisions to keep the hog pen clean, or the same hog pen and make a slip and incorporate something in his language whereby he comes to value a house more than he does his hog pen, you got a problem. He will soon be in your house.

THE THREE EVILS OF SOCIETY

ADDRESS DELIVERED BY MARTIN LUTHER KING JR.

At the National Conference on New Politics August 31, 1967
– Transcribed from an Internet Recording

Mr. Chairman, friends and brothers in this first gathering of the National Conference on New Politics. Ladies and gentlemen. . .can you hear me in the back? (No)

I don't know if the Klan is in here tonight or not with all the troubles we're having with these microphones. Seldom if ever. . ... has. . ... we're still working with it.

As I was about to say, seldom if ever has such a diverse and truly ecumenical gathering convened under the egis of politics in our nation, and I want to commend the leadership of the National Conference on New Politics for all of the great work that they have done in making this significant convention possible. Indeed, by our very nature we affirm that something new is taking place on the American political horizon. We have come here from the dusty plantations of the Deep South and the depressing ghettos of the North. We have come from the great universities and the flourishing suburbs. We have come from Appalachian poverty and from conscious stricken wealth. But we have come. And we have come here because we share a common concern for the moral health of our nation. We have come because our eyes have seen through the superficial glory and glitter of our society and observed the coming of judgment. Like the prophet of old, we have read the handwriting on the wall. We have seen our nation weighed in the balance of history and found wanting. We have come because we see this as a dark hour in the affairs of men.

For most of us this is a new mood. We are traditionally the idealists. We are the marchers from Mississippi and Selma and Washington, who staked our lives on the American Dream during the first half of this decade. Many assembled here campaigned lasciviously for Lyndon Johnson in 1964 because we could not stand idly by and watch our nation contaminated by the 18th century policies of Goldwaterism.

We were the hardcore activists who were willing to believe that Southerners could be reconstructed in the constitutional image. We were the dreamers of a dream–that dark yesterdays of man's inhumanity to man would soon be transformed into bright tomorrows of justice. Now it is hard to escape, the disillusionment and betrayal. Our hopes have been blasted and our dreams have been shattered. The promise of a Great Society was shipwrecked off the coast of Asia, on the dreadful peninsula of Vietnam. The poor, black and white, are still perishing on a lonely island of poverty in the midst of a vast ocean of material prosperity. What happens to a dream deferred? It leads to bewildering frustration and corroding bitterness.

I came to see this in a personal experience here in Chicago last summer. In all the speaking I have done in the United States before varied audiences, including some hostile whites, the only time I have ever been booed was one night in our regular weekly mass meetings by some angry young men of our movement. Now I went home that night with an ugly feeling. Selfishly I thought of my suffering and sacrifices over the last twelve years. Why would they boo one so close to them? But as I lay awake thinking. I finally came to myself. And I could not for the life of me have less impatience and understanding for those young men. For twelve years, I and others like me have held out radiant promises of progress. I had preached to them about my dream. I had lectured to them about, the not too distant day when they would have freedom, all here, now. I had urged them to have faith in America and in white society. Their hopes had soared. They were now booing me because they felt that we were unable to deliver on our promises. They were booing because we had urged them to have faith in people who had too often proved to be unfaithful. They were now hostile because they were watching the dream that they had so readily accepted, turn into a frustrating nightmare. This situation is all the more ominous, in view of the rising expectations of men the world over. The deep rumblings that we hear today, the rumblings of discontent, is the thunder of disinherited masses rising from dungeons of oppressions to the bright hills of freedom. All over the world like a fever, freedom is spreading in the widest liberation movement in history. The great masses of people are determined to end the exploitation of their races and lands. And in one majestic chorus they are singing in the worlds of our freedom song, "ain't gonna let nobody turn us around".

And so the collision course is set. The people cry for freedom and the congress attempts to legislate repression. Millions, yes billions, are appropriated for mass murder; but the most meager pittance for foreign aid for international development is crushed in the surge of reaction. Unemployment rages at a major depression level in the black ghettos, but the bipartisan response is an anti-riot bill rather than a serious poverty program. The modest proposals for model cities, rent supplement and rat control, pitiful as they were to begin with, get caught in the maze of congressional inaction. And I submit to you tonight, that a congress that proves to be more anti-negro than anti-rat needs to be dismissed. It seems that our legislative assemblies have adopted Nero as their patron saint and are bent on fiddling while our cities burn.

Even when the people persist and in the face of great obstacles, develop indigenous leadership and self-help approaches to their problems and finally tread the forest of bureaucracy to obtain existing government funds, the corrupt political order seeks to crush even this beginning of hope. The case of CDGM in Mississippi is the most publicized example but it is a story repeated many times across our nation.

Our own experience here in Chicago is especially painfully present. After an enthusiastic approval by H.E. W's Department of Adult Education, SCLC began an adult literacy project to aid 1,000 young men and women who have been pushed out of overcrowded ghetto schools, in obtaining basic [literary] skills prerequisite to receiving jobs. We had an agreement with A&P stores for 750 jobs through SCLC's job program, Operation Breadbasket and had recruited over 500 pupils the first week. At that point Congressmen Paccinski and the Daley machine intervened and demanded that Washington cut off our funds or channel them through the machine controlled poverty program in Chicago. Now we have no problem with administrative supervision, but we do have a desire to be independent of machine control and the Democratic Party patronage network. For this desire for a politically independent approach to the needs of our brothers, our funds are being stopped as of September 15th and a very meaningful program discontinued. Yes, the hour is dark, evil comes fourth in the guise of good. It is a time of double talk when men in high places have a high blood pressure of deceptive rhetoric and an anemia of concrete performance.

We cry out against welfare handouts to the poor but generously approve an oil depletion allowance to make the rich, richer. Six Mississippi plantations receive more than a million dollars a year, not to plant cotton but no provision is made to feed the tenant farmer who is put out of work by the government subsidy. The crowning achievement in hypocrisy must go to those staunch Republicans and Democrats of the Midwest and West who were given land by our government when they came here as immigrants from Europe. They were given education through the land grant colleges. They were provided with agricultural agents to keep them abreast of farming trends, they were granted low interest loans to aid in the mechanization of their farms and now that they have succeeded in becoming successful, they are paid not to farm and these are the same people that now say to black people, whose ancestors were brought to this country in chains and who were emancipated in 1863 without being given land to cultivate or bread to eat; that they must pull themselves up by their own bootstraps. What they truly advocate is Socialism for the rich and Capitalism for the poor.

I wish that I could say that this is just a passing phase in the cycles of our nation's life; certainly times of war, times of reaction throughout the society but I suspect that we are now experiencing the coming to the surface of a triple prong sickness that has been lurking within our body politic from its very beginning. That is the sickness of racism, excessive materialism and militarism. Not only is this our nation's dilemma it is the plaque of western civilization. As early as 1906 W. E.B. Dubois prophesied that the problem of the 20th century, would be the problem of the color line, now as we stand two-thirds into this crucial period of history we know full well that racism is still that hound of hell which dogs the tracks of our civilization. Ever since the birth of our nation, White America has had a Schizophrenic personality on the question of race, she has been torn between selves. A self in which, she proudly professes the great principle of democracy and a self in which she madly practices the antithesis of democracy. This tragic duality has produced a strange indecisiveness and ambivalence toward the Negro, causing America to take a step backwards simultaneously with every step forward on the question of Racial Justice; to be at once attracted to the Negro and repelled by him, to love and to hate him. There has never been a solid, unified and determined thrust to make justice a reality for Afro-Americans. The step backwards has a new name today; it is called the white backlash, but the white backlash is nothing new. It is the surfacing of old prejudices, hostilities and ambivalences that have always been there. It was caused neither by the cry of black power nor by the unfortunate recent wave of riots in our cities. The white backlash of today is rooted in the same problem that has characterized America ever since the black man landed in chains on the shores of this nation.

This does not imply that all White Americans are racist, far from it. Many white people have, through a deep moral compulsion fought long and hard for racial justice nor does it mean that America has made no progress in her attempt to cure the body politic of the disease of racism or that the dogma of racism has been considerably modified in recent years. However, for the good of America, it is necessary to refute the idea that the dominant ideology in our country, even today, is freedom and equality while racism is just an occasional departure from the norm on the part of a few bigoted extremists. Racism can well be, that corrosive evil that will bring down the curtain on western civilization.

Arnold Toynesbee has said that some twenty-six civilizations have risen upon the face of the Earth, almost all of them have descended into the junk heap of destruction. The decline and fall of these civilizations, according to Toynesbee, was not caused by external invasion but by internal decay. They failed to respond creatively to the challenges impingement upon them. If America does not respond creatively to the challenge to banish racism, some future historian will have to say, that a great civilization died because it lacked the soul and commitment to make justice a reality for all men.

The second aspect of our afflicted society is extreme materialism, an Asian writer has portrayed our dilemma in candid terms, he says, "you call your thousand material devices labor saving machinery, yet you are forever busy. With the multiplying of your machinery you grow increasingly fatigued, anxious, nervous, dissatisfied. Whatever you have you want more and wherever you are you want to go somewhere else. Your devices are neither time saving nor soul saving machinery. They are so many sharp spurs which urge you on to invent more machinery and to do more business". This tells us something about our civilization that cannot be cast aside as a prejudiced charge by an eastern thinker who is jealous of Western prosperity. We cannot escape the indictment. This does not mean that we must turn back the clock of scientific progress. No one can overlook the wonders that science has wrought for our lives. The automobile will not abdicate in favor of the horse and buggy or the train in favor of the stage coach or the tractor in favor of the hand plow or the scientific method in favor of ignorance and superstition. But our moral lag must be redeemed; when scientific power outruns moral power, we end up with guided missiles and misguided men. When we foolishly maximize the minimum and minimize the maximum we sign the warrant for our own day of doom.

It is this moral lag in our thing-oriented society that blinds us to the human reality around us and encourages us in the greed and exploitation which creates the sector of poverty in the midst of wealth. Again we have deluded ourselves into believing the myth that Capitalism grew and prospered out of the protestant ethic of hard word and sacrifice, the fact is that Capitalism was built on the exploitation and suffering of black slaves and continues to thrive on the exploitation of the poor – both black and white, both here and abroad. If Negroes and poor whites do not participate in the free flow of wealth within our economy, they will forever be poor, giving their energies, their talents and their limited funds to the consumer market but reaping few benefits and services in return. The way to end poverty is to end the exploitation of the poor, ensure them a fair share of the government services and the nation's resources. I proposed recently that a national agency be established to provide employment for everyone needing it. Nothing is more socially inexcusable than unemployment in this age. In the 30s when the nation was bankrupt it instituted such an agency, the WPA, in the present conditions of a nation glutted with resources, it is barbarous to condemn people desiring work to soul sapping inactivity and poverty. I am convinced that even this one, massive act of concern will do more than all the state police and armies of the nation to quell riots and still hatreds. The tragedy is, our materialistic culture does not possess the statesmanship necessary to do it. Victor Hugo could have been thinking of 20th Century America when he wrote, "there's always more misery among the lower classes than there is humanity in the higher classes". The time has come for America to face the inevitable choice between materialism and humanism. We must devote at least as much to our children's education and the health of the poor as we do to the care of our automobiles and the building of beautiful, impressive hotels.

We must also realize that the problems of racial injustice and economic injustice cannot be solved without a radical redistribution of political and economic power. We must further recognize that the ghetto is a domestic colony. Black people must develop programs that will aid in the transfer of power and wealth into the hands of residence of the ghetto so that they may in reality control their own destinies. This is the meaning of New Politics. People of will in the larger community, must support the black man in this effort.

The final phase of our national sickness is the disease of militarism. Nothing more clearly demonstrates our nation's abuse of military power than our tragic adventure in Vietnam. This war has played havoc with the destiny of the entire world. It has torn up the Geneva Agreement, it has seriously impaired the United Nations, it has exacerbated the hatred between continents and worst still between races. It has frustrated our development at home, telling our own underprivileged citizens that we place insatiable military demands above their critical needs. It has greatly contributed to the forces of reaction in America and strengthened the military industrial complex. And it has practically destroyed Vietnam and left thousands of Americans and Vietnamese youth maimed and mutilated and exposed the whole world to the risk of nuclear warfare. Above all, the War in Vietnam has revealed what Senator Fulbright calls, "our nation's arrogance of power". We are arrogant in professing to be concerned about the freedom of foreign nations while not setting our own house in order. Many of our Senators and Congressmen vote joyously to appropriate billions of dollars for the War in Vietnam and many of these same Senators and Congressmen vote loudly against a Fair Housing Bill to make it possible for a Negro veteran of Vietnam to purchase a decent home. We arm Negro soldiers to kill on foreign battlefields but offer little protection for their relatives from beatings and killings in our own South. We are willing to make a Negro 100% of a citizen in Warfare but reduce him to 50% of a citizen on American soil.

No war in our nation's history has ever been so violative of our conscious, our national interest and so destructive of our moral standing before the world. No enemy has ever been able to cause such damage to us as we inflict upon ourselves. The inexorable decay of our urban centers has flared into terrifying domestic conflict as the pursuit of foreign war absolves our wealth and energy. Squalor and poverty scar our cities as our military might destroy cities in a far off land to support oligarchy, to intervene in domestic conflict. The President who cherishes consensus for peace has intensified the war in answer to a cry to stop the war. It has brought tauntingly to one minutes flying time from China to a moment before the midnight of world conflagration. We are offered a tax for war instead of a plan for peace. Men of reason should no longer debate, the merits of war or means of financing war. They should end the war and restore sanity and humanity to American policy. And if the will of the people continue to be unheeded, all men of free will must create a situation in which the 1967, 68 are made a referendum on the War. The American people must have an opportunity to vote into oblivion those who cannot detach themselves from militarism, and those that lead us.

So we are here because we believe, we hope, we pray that something new might emerge in the political life of this nation which will produce a new man, new structures and new institutions and a new life for mankind. I am convinced that this new life will not emerge until our nation undergoes a radical revolution of values. When machines and computers, profit motives and property rights are considered more important than people the giant triplets of racism, economic exploitation and militarism are incapable of being conquered. A civilization can flounder as readily in the face of moral bankruptcy as it can through financial bankruptcy. A true revolution of values will soon cause us to question the fairness and justice of many of our past and present policies. We are called to play the Good Samaritan on life's road side, but that will only be an initial act. One day the whole Jericho Road must be transformed so that men and women will not be beaten and robbed as they make their journey through life. True compassion is more than flinging a coin to a beggar, it understands that an edifice which produces beggars, needs restructuring. A true revolution of values will soon look uneasily on the glaring contrast of poverty and wealth, with righteous indignation it will look at thousands of working people displaced from their jobs, with reduced incomes as a result of automation while the profits of the employers remain intact and say, this is not just. It will look across the ocean and see individual Capitalists of the West investing huge sums of money in Asia and Africa only to take the profits out with no concern for the social betterment of the countries and say, this is not just. It will look at our alliance with the landed gentry of Latin America and say, this is not just. A true revolution of values will lay hands on the world order and say of war; this way of settling differences is not just. This business of burning human beings with napalm, of filling our nation's homes with orphans and widows, of injecting poisonous drugs of hate into the veins of people normally humane, of sending men home from dark and bloodied battlefields physically handicapped and psychologically deranged cannot be reconciled with wisdom, justice and love. A nation that continues year after year, to spend more money on military defense then on programs of social uplift is approaching spiritual death.

So what we must all see is that these are revolutionary times, all over the globe, men are revolting against old systems of exploitation and out of the wombs of a frail world new systems of justice and equality are being born. The shirtless and barefoot of the Earth are rising up as never before. The people who sat in darkness have seen a great light. We in the West must support these revolutions; it is a sad fact that because of comfort, complacency, a morbid fear of Communism and our proneness to adjust to injustice, the Western nations that initiated so much of the revolutionary spirit of the modern world have now become the arch anti-revolutionaries. This has driven many to feel that only Marxism has the revolutionary spirit and in a sense, Communism is a judgment of our failure to make Democracy real and to follow through on the revolutions that we initiated. Our only hope today lies in our ability to recapture the revolutionary spirit and go out into a sometimes hostile world, declaring eternal opposition to poverty, racism and militarism. With this powerful commitment, we shall boldly challenge the status quo and unjust mores and thereby speed the day when every valley shall be exalted and every mountain and hill shall be made low and the crooked places shall be made straight and the rough places plain.

May I say in conclusion that there is a need now, more than ever before, for men and women in our nation to be creatively maladjusted. Mr. Davis said, and I say to you that I choose to be among the maladjusted, my good friend Bill Coughlin said there are those who have criticized me and many of you for taking a stand against the War in Vietnam and for seeking to say to the nation that the issues of Civil Rights cannot be separated from the issues of peace.

I want to say to you tonight that I intend to keep these issues mixed because they are mixed. Somewhere we must see that justice is indivisible, injustice anywhere is a threat to justice everywhere and I have fought to long and too hard against segregated public accommodations to end up at this point in my life, segregating my moral concerns.

So let us stand in this convention knowing that on some positions; cowardice asks the question, is it safe; expediency asks the question, is it politic; vanity asks the question, is it popular, but conscious asks the question, is it right. And on some positions, it is necessary for the moral individual to take a stand that is neither safe, nor politic nor popular; but he must do it because it is right. And we say to our nation tonight, we say to our Government, we even say to our FBI, we will not be harassed, we will not make a butchery of our conscious, we will not be intimidated and we will be heard.

References

Chapter 1 CLOAKED WITHIN

[1]   https://en.wikiquote.org/wiki/Michael_Richards
[2]   https://www.law.cornell.edu/constitution/first_amendment
[3] Medaglia, Angelica. "Amadou Diallo". The New York Times. Retrieved 2011-03-28.
[4]   http://www.history.com/topics/ku-klux-klan
[5]   https://en.wikipedia.org/wiki/Greensboro_sit-ins
[6]https://blackthen.com/back-story-this-man-narrowly-survived-iconic-lynching-that-inspired-song-strange-fruit/
[7]   http://newsone.com/2015110/kendrec-mcdade-shooting/
[8]https://www.netflix.com/title/80000770
[9]http://dailycaller.com/2014/08/18/rush-limbaugh-black-kids-being-killed-by-police-a-myth-audio/
[10]https://www.washingtonpost.com/news/post-politics/wp/2014/11/23/giuliani-white-police-officers-wouldnt-be-there-if-you-werent-killing-each-other/
[11]http://www.politifact.com/punditfact/statements/2014/dec/04/bill-oreilly/bill-oreilly-cites-faulty-data-claim-about-shootin/
[12]   https://m.youtube.com/watch?v=xUlqTNwm-mk

Chapter 2 OMEGA THEORY

[1]http://www.tv.com/shows/dog-the-bounty-hunter/community/
[2]   https://en.wikipedia.org/wiki/Death_of_Eric_Garner
[3]http://www.nbcnews.com/storyline/michael-brown-shooting/killing-unarmed-teen-what-we-know-about-browns-death-n178696
[4]https://www.justice.gov/sites/default/files/opa/press-releases/attachments/2015/03/04/doj_report_on_shooting_of_michael_brown_1.pdf
[5]   https://en.wikipedia.org/wiki/Shooting_of_Tamir_Rice
[6]https://en.wikipedia.org/wiki/Death_of_Freddie_Gray
[7]https://en.wikipedia.org/wiki/Death_of_Sandra_Bland
[8]http://www.cnn.com/2016/09/15/us/sandra-bland-wrongful-death-settlement/index.html
[9]https://en.wikipedia.org/wiki/Death_in_custody
[10] http://gun.laws.com/state-gun-laws/louisiana-gun-laws
[11]http://distracteddriveraccidents.com/biking-and-driving-with-earbuds-illegal-in-california/

[12]   http://www.nydailynews.com/news/national/king-cops-killed-noel-aguilar-face-murder-charge-article-1.2474083
[13]http://abcnews.go.com/US/dash-cam-video-clears-nj-man-violent-traffic/story?id=22660928
[14]https://en.wikipedia.org/wiki/Shooting_of_Philando_Castile
[15]http://www.nydailynews.com/news/national/philando-castile-stopped-cops-52-times-14-years-article-1.2705348
[16]http://www.nydailynews.com/news/politics/de-blasio-reeling-minnesota-louisiana-police-killings-article-1.2702863
[17]http://pittsburgh.cbslocal.com/video/category/spoken-word-kdkatv/3427835-report-officers-shot-during-dallas-protest-over-fatal-police-shootings/
[18]http://www.bing.com/videos/search?q=our+profession+is+hurting&src=IE-TopResult&conversationid=&ru=%2fsearch%3fq%3dour%2bprofession%2bis%2bhurting%26src%3dIE-TopResult%26FORM%3dIETR02%26conversationid%3d&view=detail&mmscn=vwrc&mid=9825DDA6B3E50CE959989825DDA6B3E50CE95998&FORM=WRVORC
[19]http://www.nbcnews.com/news/us-news/oklahoma-man-eric-harris-fatally-shot-police-accident-instead-tased-n340116
[20]   https://en.wikipedia.org/wiki/Shooting_of_Walter_Scott
[21]http://www.nbcnews.com/news/us-news/tyre-king-13-fatally-shot-police-columbus-ohio-n648671
[22]http://www.cnn.com/2016/09/20/us/oklahoma-tulsa-police-shooting/index.html
[23]http://www.nydailynews.com/news/national/police-release-video-keith-lamont-scott-shooting-graphic-article-1.2817830
[24]https://dailystormer.name/whackjobs-at-the-un-defend-sniper-attacks-say-us-is-racist/

Additional Sources
https://en.wikipedia.org/wiki/Shooting_of_Michael_Brown
https://en.wikipedia.org/wiki/Shooting_of_Alton_Sterling
http://www.cnn.com/2016/07/06/us/baton-rouge-shooting-alton-sterling/index.html
https://www.justice.gov/usao-mdla/pr/united-states-attorney-announces-federal-criminal-investigation-death-alton-sterling
http://www.usatoday.com/story/news/nation/2016/07/06/black-leaders-demand-state-probe-fatal-shooting-baton-rouge-police/86745562/
http://socialistworker.org/2015/03/23/a-family-keeps-the-struggle-alive

http://www.nytimes.com/2016/07/08/us/philando-castile-falcon-heights-shooting.html?_r=0
http://www.cnn.com/videos/us/2016/07/08/police-officers-shot-dallas-texas-sot-ctn.cnn

Chapter 3 THE PARETO PRINCIPLE
[1]https://www.youtube.com/watch?v=C6pymcUV8v4 (fuhrman tapes)
[2]https://en.wikipedia.org/wiki/September_11_attacks
[3]https://www.npr.org/sections/thetwo-way/2016/07/08/485220431/were-hurting-dallas-police-chief-david-brown-says
[4]https://en.wikipedia.org/wiki/Shooting_of_Laquan_McDonald
[5]http://newsone.com/3513579/chicagos-top-cop-seeks-to-break-the-code-of-silence/ (false reports)
[6]http://www.ajc.com/news/national/ohio-police-officer-nakia-jones-voices-outrage-over-alton-sterling-shooting-with-powerful-facebook-message/9QauqQfuklFM03wlZHSbNM/
[7]http://www.huffingtonpost.com/2015/06/16/baltimore-joe-crystal_n_7582374.html
[8]http://www.nytimes.com/2016/07/13/us/the-new-officer-friendly-armed-with-instagram-tweets-and-emojis.html?_r=0
[9]http://www.cbc.ca/news/web-extra-the-game-s-good-cop-1.3815668
[10]https://en.wikipedia.org/wiki/Queensbridge_Houses
[11]http://www.nydailynews.com/new-york/queens/dozens-drug-dealing-suspects-nabbed-queens-housing-projects-article-1.1348526

Additional Sources
http://www.cnn.com/2015/11/24/us/chicago-laquan-mcdonald-shooting-video/

Chapter 5 CODE ICE
[1]http://gawker.com/5577713/report-mel-gibson-uses-n-word-threatens-rape-of-wife

[2]https://theintercept.com/2016/06/07/tased-in-the-chest-for-23-seconds-dead-for-8-minutes-now-facing-a-lifetime-of-recovery/
[3]http://www.huffingtonpost.com/entry/timothy-runnels-bryce-masters-Taser_us_57571f6de4b07823f95188c9   (video)

Chapter 6 Blue Law

[1]https://jezebel.com/congratulations-to-paula-deen-on-her-new-book-deal-with-1688934777
[2]https://archive.org/stream/WillieLynchLetter1712/the_willie_lynch_letter_the_making_of_a_slave_1712_djvu.txt

[3]https://www.miamiherald.com/news/local/crime/article213647764.html#storylink=cpy

[4]https://www.miamiherald.com/news/local/crime/article212948924.html
[5]https://www.encyclopediavirginia.org/_An_act_concerning_Servants_and_Slaves_1705 {At #34}
[6]http://www.blackpast.org/primary/louisianas-code-noir-1724 {At #27}
[7]https://en.wikipedia.org/wiki/Treatment_of_slaves_in_the_United_States#cite_ref-Lasgrayt,_Deborah_1999_40-0   {Punishment and Abuse Section at footnote #40}
[8]https://www.vox.com/identities/2017/5/1/15499996/jordan-edwards-police-shooting-texas-balch-springs
[9]   https://caselaw.findlaw.com/us-supreme-court/490/386.html
[10]http://www.governing.com/topics/public-justice-safety/gov-california-police-lethal-force-legal-standard.html
[11]   https://en.wikipedia.org/wiki/Community_policing
[12]http://www.cleveland.com/court-justice/index.ssf/2014/12/justice_department_recommends.html
[13]Michelle Alexander "The New Jim Crow" (The New Press, 2010) at page 100
[14]https://www.cnn.com/2017/07/12/us/florida-state-attorney-aramis-ayala-traffic-stop/index.html
[15]http://americancreation.blogspot.com/2009/08/jeffersons-tree-of-liberty-quote-in.html

Additional Sources
https://www.yahoo.com/news/florida-police-chief-instructed-officers-214245993.html
http://plsonline.eku/edu/insidelook/history-policing-united-states-part-1 through 6 Entire section
Social Psychology: Theories, Research, and Applications by Robert S. Feldman
https://www.simplypsychology.org/milgram.html
http://www.cleveland.com/metro/index.ssf/2015/01/tanisha_anderson_was_restraine.html
https://www.cnn.com/2015/05/05/us/rough-ride-lawsuits-freddie-gray/index.html
Crossman, Ashley. "The Concept of Social Structure in Our Society." ThoughtCo, Dec. 31, 2017, thoughtco.com/social-structure-defined-3026594
Crossman, Ashley. "The Definition of Social Control." "ThoughtCo, Jan.15, 2018, thoughtco.com/social-control-3026587
Cole, Nicki Lisa, Ph.D. "What is Social Stratification, and Why Does It Matter?" ThoughtCo, Oct. 17, 2017, thoughtco.com/what-is-social-stratification-3026643
https://en.wikipedia.org/wiki/Tulsa_race_riot
http://www.scribd.com/doc/134362247/Martin-Luther-King-Jr-The-Three-Evils-of-Society-1967
https://eprints.lse.ac.uk/22514/1/2308Ramadams.pdf
http://wolffacts.org/wolf-pack-hierarchy.html
https://www.nytimes.com/2016/07/10/us/dallas-quiet-after-police-shooting-but-protests-flare-elsewhere.html

Chapter 7 We the People

[1]http://www.scribd.com/doc/134362247/Martin-Luther-King-Jr-The-Three-Evils-of-Society-1967

CPSIA information can be obtained
at www.ICGtesting.com
Printed in the USA
LVHW081304290119
605649LV00014B/175/P